080
P945bj

Sapulpa Public Library
27 W. Dewey Ave.
Sapulpa, OK 74066-3909

Journeys

Journeys

Prosateurs

Journeys is a collection of fiction and nonfiction works.

In the works of fiction, names, places, and incidents are either products of the author's imagination or are used fictitiously. Any resemblance to actual events, locales, businesses, or any persons, living or dead, is strictly coincidental.

In the works of nonfiction, no warranties are expressed or implied. Authors are responsible for the accuracy of their respective works. Links were valid at the time of publication, but may change. Further, the publisher assumes no responsibility for content on author or third party websites.

Copyright 2022 by Prosateurs. Individual works copyright 2022 by each respective author. All rights reserved. No part of this book may be reproduced in any form or by any electronic or mechanical means, including information storage and retrieval systems, without written permission, except by a reviewer who may quote brief passages in a review.

Cover photo and interior graphics © depositphotos.com. All rights reserved. Approved for use in accordance to their guidelines.

Trademarks and advertising slogans used in this book belong to their respective companies.

ISBN 978-1-387-87782-9

Printed in the United States of America

10 9 8 7 6 5 4 3 2 1

Dedicated to all of you
who have survived
& even flourished
in these uncertain times.
May your journeys
be joyous.

Contents

Articles & Essays
Country Cooking *by Heath Stallcup* — 1
From the Wild, With Love *by D.E. Chandler* — 3
Hair Today; Gone Tomorrow *by Stephen B. Bagley* — 6
Jawing About Java *by Stephen B. Bagley* — 9
The Power of No *by Stephen B. Bagley* — 12

Devotionals
Big Table God *by Stephen B. Bagley* — 13
Broken Cup *by Stephen B. Bagley* — 15
Character *by Kathy Akins* — 16
Life Interrupted *by Kathy Akins* — 17
Renewal *by Stephen B. Bagley* — 18
Roll in the Grass *by Kathy Akins* — 19
Seek Good *by Wendy Blanton* — 20
Strength in Christ *by Kathy Akins* — 21
The Measure of Success *by Wendy Blanton* — 22
The Tenacity of a Weed *by Wendy Blanton* — 23

Memoirs
Even the Old Were Young Once *by Kathy Akins* — 24
Lessons from Chicago *by Wendy Blanton* — 28
Trapped in a Castle *by Debbie Anderson* — 30

Poems
A Mirror, Forlorn *by D.E. Chandler* — 36
Carroll after Dark *by D.E. Chandler* — 37
High Maintenance *by Stephen B. Bagley* — 38
Lost *by Kathy Akins* — 39
Oppenhiemer *by D.E. Chandler* — 40
Personal Armageddon *by Stephen B. Bagley* — 41
Prodigal *by Kathy Akins* — 42
Whispers *by Stephen B. Bagley* — 43

Recipes
Arda, the Dragonriders' Drink *by Wendy Blanton* — 44
Biscuits and Gravy *by Heath Stallcup* — 45
Chicken and Dumplings *by Heath Stallcup* — 47
Chocolate Bonbons *by Joanne Verbridge* — 49

Recipes Continued
Chocolate Crinkles *by Joanne Verbridge*	50
Cordon Bleu Roll-ups *by Debbie Anderson*	51
Depression Buttermilk Biscuits *by Joanne Verbridge*	53
Italian Beef Sandwiches *by Debbie Anderson*	54
No Salt, Please *by Debbie Anderson*	57

Short Stories
Mole Hunt *by Kathy Akins*	58
Rapunzel: A Love Story *by Debbie Anderson*	61
That's No Bull *by Kathy Akins*	69
The End of a Story *by Stephen B. Bagley*	73
The Helper *by Wendy Blanton*	76
The Tree King and the Stone Girl *by D.E. Chandler*	87

Excerpts from Books
Dawn Before The Dark by Wendy Blanton	90
Murder by the Acre by Stephen B. Bagley	97
Nova Wave by D.E. Chandler	101

About the Authors   107

Prosateurs is a group of authors and poets whose main focus is to publish our works via traditional and non-traditional venues. Visit Prosateurs.blogspot.com for more information.

Country Cooking
By Heath Stallcup

'COUNTRY' DOESN'T NECESSARILY MEAN the South or 'Southern.' You can live in the depths of the largest city and still enjoy country cooking. Whether it's a big pot of greens or cornbread and beans or biscuits and gravy, it's those 'stick to your ribs' type of foods that bring us comfort. Those foods that we remember from our youth.

As a child, I stood in the kitchen with my grandma and watched as she cooked. I'd ask her, why do this or why do that, and if there was a specific reason, she'd share. If not, she'd shake her head and tell me 'that's the way it's done.'

These days, folks are all about the healthy eatin'. Every day I read about folks who followed what the latest trends in eating were and how they died at such a young age, usually of heart disease.

Remember when they told us for years that eggs were LOADED in cholesterol? How unhealthy they were? Entire industries popped up to counteract those unhealthy protein bombs that slide out a chicken's butt.

Containers full of nothing but egg whites, artificial egg products that had the excess cholesterol chemically removed. Powdered eggs that were supposedly more healthy for you. Only to have it all come crashing down when the truth was quietly revealed…eggs are fine. Your body converts the cholesterol in the eggs into energy rather than injecting straight cholesterol into your veins to clog your heart.

Remember when bacon was deemed the devil because of the fat content? Not to mention all of the evil salts and flavorings. For years people forced themselves to eat turkey bacon or veggie bacon.

Then about twenty years ago, there was a series of studies performed and they quietly announce, well, bacon doesn't kill you. In fact, other than it tastes so good that people want to overeat it, there's really nothing wrong with it. Your body converts the fats into energy and doesn't inject it straight into your veins and kill you.

Meanwhile, country folks were eating bacon and eggs for breakfast. Swallowing it down with fresh, whole milk that came nearly straight from the cow. Drinking real orange juice and mopping it all up with honest to god biscuits with real butter and homemade jelly.

These poor, ignorant, uneducated folks only lived to their nineties or such. These poor country folks had no idea they were doing it all wrong. Or were they?

Real butter. SALTED butter…instead of margarine. Whole milk not skim. Bacon. From a pig…not a bird or a cucumber. Eggs. Real eggs from a chicken. Bacon grease instead of hydrogenated vegetable oil. Fresh fruits and vegetables from their own garden rather than the corporate farms that mass produce everything. And the food was FANTASTIC. It tasted like…HOME.

You walked away from the table feeling full, not feeling like something was missing. And these country folks were outliving all of those people who were listening to the experts that told them that real food was bad for them.

Maybe it's time to get back to our roots. Growing as much of your own food as you can. You don't have to live on a farm to do that either. During World War II, people were encouraged to grow Victory Gardens. Even if all you have is a small flower bed, plant vegetables. If you have a back yard, stake out a plot and grow your own stuff. It may not be as pretty as the stuff you buy in the grocery store (the stuff with blemishes are usually sold to canneries rather than placed on the shelf for you to see) but the explosion of flavor cannot be beat.

Try it yourself. Just grow one tomato plant. You'll get multiple fruit from it and when compared to those pale examples you find in the grocery store? Your mouth will thank you. The difference in flavors is amazing.

Or…try this. Find a place that sells 'farm' eggs. I'm talking real farm eggs, not the 'organic, free range, brown shelled' five dollar a dozen examples in your local supermarket.

Once you've found some, crack it open into a dish. In another dish, crack open a store egg. The first thing you'll notice is the yolks. Farm eggs have this deep orange yolk, and the store egg has an almost fluorescent yellow yolk. Don't be alarmed. It's not radioactive. But the pale yellow example is what you've been eating all of this time.

Now, toss some butter in your pan, heat it up and fry them both up. However you like it, but know that real men eat them over easy to over medium. Runny yolks, y'all. You need something to sop up with your biscuits.

Notice the difference in flavor? Yeah. THAT'S what I'm talking about. I think you'll find getting back to our country roots is healthy and delicious. Try it. You wouldn't be sorry.

From the Wild, With Love
By D.E. Chandler

I ONCE WROTE A BLOG POST about cleaning wild onions in the spring. This is the result of a much longer meditation on the subject.

They have all grown up together. Possibly from the seed of some long dead parent. They have divided and divided again, each giving up a part of itself to create a separate living being. Each of these living beings is nestled close against another until suddenly one day the earth itself is torn apart, and they are lifted from their home. Their next experience is akin to drowning. They are submerged in water, and what little earth clings to their roots is ripped away in the current created by their passing. Some alien force has gripped them and dragged them together through this tumult and stinging surge.

From the perspective of the wild onions it must be a terrifying way to die.

From my perspective, it is ritual. It is a meditation. As I rinse the wild onions and prepare to "clean" them I contemplate my own place in the multiverse and the generations of people—mainly women—from a time lost to time to this very day, who have done much the same dance every spring. Once the smells of coffee and bacon fade, but even before the chickens are fed and watered, the onions must be dug from the ground, but that is the easy part.

After tending the animals, the onions must have an initial rinse, to get rid of most of the dirt. Then the hard part begins. They must be separated into individual plants to remove any tiny non-onion plants that have crept into the colony. It is supremely important to separate these, and eliminate any possibility of encroachment by toxic plants like the death camas, or crow poison. No one wants to end up in the hospital. The root end of each minuscule (most no bigger than the head of a hat pin) onion bulb must be trimmed off. Once the root is trimmed off, usually with fingernails or a paring knife, the old skins and dead outer leaves must be carefully peeled away. It is long and tedious work. For a dozen eggs, we use about three or four handfuls of onions, each handful about the diameter of a half-dollar. Upwards of five-hundred or so plants. Just to get a mess of onions worthy of scrambling into a dozen eggs takes up the entire morning, but that time is precious.

It is perhaps especially precious in the post-millennial world, where every second seems to be appointed to some function of the mind. The mind is kept so busy that it is rare to find moments for it to unfurl and allow the imagination some breathing room. In this space, now, that is precisely what happens. My mind begins to relax, and I find a sort of presence with the task that also allows me to examine my own thoughts.

Not only do I examine the possibility of the generations gone, I also daydream about the generations to come. Will my grandchildren remember the wild onion and teach their grandchildren? I contemplate the spring morning all around me. I hear—and listen to—the birds, domestic and wild. I imagine what is happening in each of their lives.

Where will that woodpecker take the tender morsel he has wrested from the light pole? What is the guinea in the run squawking about now? Is the turkey gobbling because he's upset, or because it's spring and he's feeling his oats? How many killdeer have I seen dart across the field?

The wind is mild and from the south today. It is blowing away the storms from the week just passing. It is sweet with the scent of wild plum and henbit, dead nettle and spring beauty, tulip and grape hyacinth. All the while there is the rhythm developing: pinch or cut, pull, peel, rinse, peel some more, rinse again. Once each onion has had its initial cleaning, which I call its outside cleaning, the whole mess is taken indoors, given a good final wash in the sink, and then aligned. This part is important, if you want anything resembling uniformity in chopping the onions.

By the time these things are done, it is time for lunch (or dinner, depending on the day,) and the chickens are laying. What eggs there are, I gather and add to yesterday's eggs to make up the dozen. A surprising sense of accomplishment comes now from knowing I am creating something for the ones I love. This will be something from the chickens we have tended, and from nature who is ever abundant. A dish of food to nourish them—in body, mind, and spirit. A dish of love.

The onions are then separated into small bundles, chopped, and sautéed in lots of butter. Sometime just after they start browning and before they burn, the eggs must be added. In the name of authenticity, these should be as fresh as possible. They will be washed (as we don't wash eggs beforehand) cracked individually into a small bowl and then added to a large bowl. Once all eggs are cleaned, cracked and added to the larger bowl, I will beat them with milk, salt, and pepper to get them ready for the pan. When the onions just start to brown, I add the eggs and scramble them as usual.

It is interesting, but a little disconcerting that this writing is so short while the process is so very long. I guess in a way, you really have to be there. Like snapping beans on the front porch in the height of summer, it is something that is impossible to capture with the same weight, the same emotion. This won't stop me trying.

There is much I still have to learn about homesteading, and I hope there are many more opportunities to clean onions for family dinner, taking the entire morning to just exist, to just meditate on the importance of wild onions, dedication to process, and love.

Hair Today, Gone Tomorrow
By Stephen B. Bagley

MY HAIR DOES THIS ALBERT EINSTEIN thing in the morning, wild and crazy, which is amazing considering I basically just have three hairs on the top of my head, one is red, one is gray, and one is green—which would worry me except for my habit of scratching my head with whatever pen I'm using and lately I've been using one with green ink.

Anyway, my hair does its own wild thang in the morning, and while I could complain and long for that tousled handsome hairstyle that male models and movie stars spend thousands of dollars achieving, I am glad I still have those few, bravely hanging on without many of their brethren to support them.

It reminds me of Luke 12:7 which says God keeps track of how many hairs we have: "But even the very hairs of your head are all numbered. Fear not therefore: ye are of more value than many sparrows." As my hair leaves me, I like to think that I'm helping God cut back on His counting, freeing up a bit of His time to maybe enjoy a glass of Dr Pepper.

On the value of sparrows compared to humans, they are quarrelsome, greedy, and lustfully stupid. Sparrows, on the other hand, seem quite nice, but I don't know much about them. However, when you get boastful and go around bragging that you're worth more than many sparrows, remember that the verse doesn't say you're worth more than many dogs or cats. Don't be so full of yourself, buddy.

I don't think sparrows have to worry about feather loss, either. I mean, sparrows have lots of worries and I don't want to minimize their trauma, but preventing the loss of their feathers doesn't seem to be a multi-billion dollar industry as it is for preventing baldness in humans. Bird brains may be wiser than human brains in this regard.

As far back as 4,000 BC, people were searching for cures for hair loss. The Egyptians, for instance, had a cure where the physician ground up donkey hooves, dates, oil, and other ingredients that I don't want to talk about, cooked the mixture, and then rubbed the resulting mess on their patients' balding heads. I could not find any testimonials about the potion's effectiveness, but I imagine it's hard to write an advertisement in hieroglyphics.

Another Egyptian medical prescription dating from around 1500 BC said you should mix the fat from a hippo, snake, crocodile, and other animals and then plaster the goop on your scalp. If the mixture doesn't work—shocking possibility—then boil porcupine hair and apply to the bald areas while warm. This was to be done for four days, after which the patient was probably quite willing to be bald to avoid the cure.

Nearly twelve hundred years later, the fabled physician and philosopher Hippocrates swore the cure for hair loss was a mix of opium, beet root, horseradish, various spices, and—in a daring pharmaceutical move—pigeon droppings! One wonders if they actually put the opium on the head or simply gave it to the patient so he wouldn't care that bird poop was on his head. This smelly concoction, however, was not universally accepted. The philosopher Aristotle said Hippocrates was WRONG about the pigeon dropping and that goat urine was the ideal treatment. At last, a sensible suggestion!

Around 50 BC, Romans who suffered hair loss rubbed myrrh onto their scalps. At least, this doesn't involve animal droppings and urine, but worse recipes floated around. For instance, Queen Cleopatra told the balding Julius Caesar to grind dead mice and horse teeth with bear grease to apply to his head. I'm not sure Cleo wasn't pranking him.

In China, thousands of years of medicine led them to this traditional medicine solution: Blend rosemary, safflower oil, herbs, and...dear me...crushed animal...ah...private parts to be applied to the balding areas.

In Scandinavia, those Viking scallywags rubbed goose poop into the scalps to deal with hair loss. It didn't work, but since the Vikings were quick to take offense and quicker to swing an axe, I doubt anyone made fun of their shiny poopy pates.

Later on, over in merry old England, Henry VIII, he of the many unhappy wives, also was afflicted with hair loss. He fought his receding hairline with the latest scientific ointment made of...sigh...dog and horse urine.

The United States has the dubious honor of using 19th and 20th century pseudo-science to create possibly lethal hair treatments. This included such advances as:

• A helmet that delivered electric jolts to various locations on the scalp. If your hair didn't grow, you were to increase the duration and voltage until you got results. It was probably better if you handled the controls yourself. Best if you didn't do it at all.

- Another helmet that exposed the scalp to the "miracle of radium." The burns and cancer were a (terrible) bonus.
- Various elixirs, including ones made of "sacred soil," lead powder, and, once again, urine from people and animals. I don't know how urine ever got connected with hair growth, but it makes as much sense as bird droppings. Both are gross.

All the potions, liniments, and elixirs to cure various aliments were called snake oil since the early mixtures were supposed to contain oil extracted from various snakes. Most were based on mineral oil, and almost none actually contained any parts of snakes. Many of these would disappear in the years after the 1906 Pure Food and Drug Act and the eventual creation of the Food and Drug Administration. Oddly enough, oil from Chinese water snakes contains high levels of eicosapentaenoic acid (one of the two types of omega-3 fatty acids most readily used by our bodies) and might benefit people who suffer from joint pain and may be good for dry, damaged hair. If nothing else, it's a great conversation starter: "Guess what I've got on my hair? I'll give you a hint. Think Medusa."

Not all treatments for hair loss were icky. In 1896, the Scientific American magazine published an article about how music could be used to increase hair growth, but not just any music would work. String instruments such as violins and pianos benefited hair while brass instruments damaged hair. Considering the number of hair bands in the Eighties, I'm assuming loud glam rock helps hair grow even though it eventually causes tone deafness.

Science continues to work on ways to regrow hair and stop hair loss with various drugs and treatments. Maybe one day soon, my three hairs will greet many returnees with much rejoicing. Until then, I guess I'll wear a hat.

Jawing About Java
By Stephen B. Bagley

I DON'T CLAIM TO BE a huge coffee drinker. One cup a day is about my limit although I have indulged in two or three once in a while and thus did not sleep for a couple of days. I have friends, however, who have built up such a tolerance for coffee that they drink 10 cups a day and—other than a tendency to vibrate and *talkveryfastlikethis*—seem fine if a bit wide-eyed and excitable especially since they can see air.

Coffee consumption has been called the most common addiction in the world. And other than the desire to tell our fellow humans that their personal life choices are wrong, it probably is. According to the International Coffee Organization, the average American goes through 11 pounds of coffee a year. Which seems like a lot until you learn the average person in Finland consumes 27.5 pounds yearly. This explains their language, which is actually English but sped up 1,000 times.

As of 2020, coffee was the second most traded commodity in the world, second only to crude oil with the coffee industry being worth more than 100 billion dollars a year. That's a lot of beans. Except coffee beans aren't beans. They're the seeds of the coffee fruit which grows on a big bush. The seeds happen to look like legumes. But how did we go from a pinto bean lookalike to a hot steaming mug of jitter juice?

No one really knows. Several legends attempt to explain how coffee became a cherished drink. My favorite is about Khalid, an Ethiopian goat herder in the 9th century, who noticed his goats were consuming fruit from a bush. His four-footed herd became energized, running and jumping with joy even though they were fated to end up on a table in *kai wat* (a spicy stew for those who don't speak Ethiopian including me). He told a local monk about his herd's behavior. The monk made a drink out of the fruit and found it helped keep him awake during nightly prayer sessions.

Another legend says that one Sheikh Omar, a faith healer, discovered coffee. He had been exiled to a desert cave for dallying with a king's wife. Soon, he began to starve. Desperate, he tried eating the berries from a nearby bush, but they were too bitter. He roasted the berries, but that made them too hard to eat. Then he boiled them which produced a brown liquid that he drank, and he was filled with vigor. The coffee kept him alive for days. When this story spread, the exile edict was lifted, and Omar returned and was made a saint for his discovery. A monastery was built in his honor. Poor Khalid was neglected, but that's often the case with goat herders as many of you know. There's another tale about a man—Yemenite Sufi mystic Ghothul Akbar Nooruddin Abu al-Hasan al-Shadhili; I'm sure he had a shorter nickname—who ate the berries after he saw highly active birds eating them, but let's move on.

Around the 15th century, we have the first written mention of coffee in Yemen whose citizens had learned of the liquid from Ethiopia. Consumption of the drink spread and reached Venice in the 16th century and the rest of Europe thereafter, particularly after Pope Clement VIII baptized it. Yes, that's right. Coffee was baptized by a pope. When coffee reached the Christian world, many clergymen regarded it as "Satan's drink" since it came from predominately Muslim countries that had been at war with Christendom for centuries. The pope was asked to ban it, but he refused to do so until he had tasted it. He took a sip and supposedly said, "This devil's drink is delicious. We should cheat the devil by baptizing it." With his blessing, coffee aficionados enjoyed cups of joe without fearing for their immortal souls.

Even the United States has history with the drink. Tea was the favored beverage for the Thirteen Colonies, but after the Boston Tea Party, Britain cut off the tea supplies because King George and Parliament were jerks. So the Americans took up coffee instead. When the war was over and tea supplies restored, coffee remained the drink for the American breakfast. Before that, hard cider and beer were the breakfast beverages, *even for children*. Ah, America, so intoxicatingly free and so freely intoxicated.

Speaking of the United States, delicious *kona* coffee is our gift to the world of coffee. It is only grown in Hawaii and, more recently, California. But our largest contribution to the coffee drinking world may be Starbucks® which began in Seattle in 1971. Starbucks has grown until it has more than 34,000 locations in the world with around 17,000 in the United States in 2022. It is also where you can get a cup of java with more calories than a cheeseburger and fries.

Not that coffee itself has any calories. The calories come from sugar, whole milk, 2% milk, soy milk, oat milk, coconut milk, light cream, heavy cream, whipped cream, ice cream, caramel, chocolate syrup, chocolate sprinkles, chocolate chips, vanilla syrup, spices...

Really, it might be easier to list what people don't want in their coffee. Turnips. They don't want turnips. Yet.

Coffee does have plenty of caffeine. A regular eight-ounce cup of black coffee has between 95 to 200 milligrams of caffeine while one can of regular cola has about 23 to 35 milligrams. Decaf coffee contains two to 12 milligrams. Curious fact: the caffeine removed from decaffeinated coffee is sold to cola and pharmaceutical companies. Energy drinks have surpassed coffee's ability to deliver the jolts with one brand offering 500 milligrams per eight ounces. It should come with a defibrillator.

Not that coffee has completely given up the caffeine battle. Espresso (not eXpresso, you Philistines) carries 484 milligrams per eight ounces, although almost no one sane drinks eight ounces at one sitting. Instead, it's served in shot glasses. I was going to explain how to make it, but life is too short. There is a Starbucks near you, possibly next door or in your garage. Give them your credit card, and they will brew one for you and serve it in a non-specific holiday cup.

One last coffee fact: it was probably an alcoholic beverage first. Scholars think that coffee fruit was fermented to make a drink from which coffee arose. The word 'coffee' comes from the Arabic word for wine: *qahwah*, a mulled wine, which later became *kahveh* in Turkish, and then *koffie* in Dutch, leading us to the English word 'coffee.'

So as you sip your grande macchiato with whole milk, extra espresso, two presses of vanilla syrup, caramel drizzle, whipped cream, and nutmeg and chocolate sprinkles on top, think of Khalid as you enjoy the bitter brew of mystics and kings.

The Power of No
By Stephen B. Bagley

"No" means "no" is a lesson we should all learn if we haven't already. You might be surprised to learn, however, that it can be useful in all sorts of ways.

"Drink and drive."
"No."
"Ignore the process of science."
"No."
"Ignore the results of medical research."
"No."
"Take on duty that isn't yours."
"No."
"Feel shame for being you."
"No."
"Laugh at a racist joke."
"NO!"
"Believe women aren't the equal of men in all ways."
"NO!"
"Deny God or even the existence of something in the universe more powerful than humanity."
"NO!"
"Enjoy that double dip ice cream Sundae even though your diabetes doctors say you shouldn't.
"Sigh. No."
"Hate people just because they are different from you."
"No. *No.* **No.**"
"Accept responsibility for something that isn't your fault."
"No."
"Deny responsibility for things that are your fault."
"No."
"Eat turnips."
"NO! A THOUSAND TIMES, NO!"

You might find a good, moral, intelligent "no" could really improve your life. It will at least keep you from having to eat turnips.

Big Table God
By Stephen B. Bagley

"Blessed is the man who will eat at the feast in the kingdom of God."—Luke 14:15.

MY GOD IS A BIG TABLE GOD. He has an infinitely-sized table at which everyone is welcome, no matter skin color, ethnicity, looks, gender, denomination, political bend, environmental views, almost-anything-we-think-divides-us. It's a huge table filled with good eats, and at this table, people are laughing and talking and sharing and they're waiting for you.

Some people serve a Tiny Table God. You have to be the correct color, hold the correct political views, and be the correct gender to sit at that table. You have to be biased against the other people, all those who are different from the so-called correct. Your sins have to be the acceptable sins, the ones that they themselves might indulge in. All other people—they must stand by and starve as they watch the acceptable ones gorge themselves. The starving people might protest, but fortunately, a good-sized Bible makes a great club if a person wants to use it like that.

That's not the Big Table God.

That's not my God.

It's the Tiny Table God.

You might be familiar with the Tiny Table God. He's vengeful, shallow, bigoted, judgmental, self-righteous, quick-to-anger, and terrible in His fury, the heavy-handed father whose children cringe at His approach. Because we've created so many gods in the past, we think this God should conform. He should support who we vote for, shower forgiveness only on those we find worthy, and grant prosperity and good health only to the right people. We loudly preach of His miracles, but in the same breath, we deny His endless grace, boundless mercy, and infinite power. He's beyond our understanding, and we resent it and attempt to force Him into a box that we can control and understand. Except...God won't be put into any human box.

No, he's a Big Table God.

At His Big Table, you will see all sorts of people, many that might surprise you, but all of them are His children. Over there gather the

Assembly of God and the Baptists, next to the Methodists and Episcopalians, and they're sharing countless, marvelous casseroles. The Catholics offer fantastic Mexican and Italian dishes with plenty to share. Must not forget to mention the Latter Day Saints who never let an attendee to a church dinner go hungry. The Greek Orthodox are waving us over for *dolma* and *moussaka*. The Asian church folk graciously offer *nikuman, pad krapow gai,* and *sinangag*. So many nationalities, so different, but all the same at heart. They're all part of the church of the Big Table. People are everywhere and sharing everything, including warm hugs and lots of true love. There's singing and talking and endless introductions to people who are delighted to know the real you.

But of course, you know who's sitting at the head of the table, the Host of All Creation. He's smiling and laughing, and He's waiting for you to join Him.

He's beckoning you over.

God is waiting for you.

"For God so loved (you) the world that He gave his one and only Son (Jesus Christ), that whoever believes in Him (you) shall not perish but have eternal life."—John 3:16.

Come sit at His table.

Broken Cup
By Stephen B. Bagley

"He heals the brokenhearted and bandages their wounds."—Psalm 147:2

THE JAPANESE PRACTICE AN ART called *Kintsugi*, which means 'golden joinery' or 'golden repair.' They take broken pottery and repair it by mending the breakage with glue or lacquer mixed with powdered gold, silver, or platinum.

The philosophy behind this says there is beauty in the history of a broken piece, that the breakage and the repair enhance the uniqueness of each item. Many times, the repair is stronger and more beautiful than the original material.

"We are all broken," I once heard a speaker say. He said we should all acknowledge our brokenness. That is true, but it's not enough to simply be broken; being broken is easy and all too common. It is the healing that is hard, that takes work and commitment. If we want a more abundant life, however, we can't stay broken. We must seek healing.

Of all the miracles recorded in the Bible, some of the most powerful involved healing of the body and the mind. Jesus Christ wants to heal the damage of this life. He wants to soothe all the pain and sorrow that daily living inflicts on us. We are all broken cups, and He wants to heal our hearts and spirits with His precious mercy and love.

My prayer is that each of us will seek this healing of our hearts. We might be broken, but with His miraculous help, we can be strong, beautiful, and triumphant in our broken places.

Character
By Kathy Akins

***"But the Lord said unto Samuel, Look not on his countenance, or on the height of his stature; because I have refused him: for the Lord seeth not as man seeth; for man looketh on the outward appearance, but the Lord looketh on the heart."*—1 Samuel 16:7**

IT IS HARD TO GET past a first impression when we meet someone new. Especially if that person makes a less than stellar impression. We aren't supposed to judge people based on appearance, but humans have a hard time with that. I usually try to follow my dogs lead on things. They often have a better instinct when it comes to people.

Even the prophet Samuel struggled with allowing the outer man to sway his opinion. When the people of Israel cried out to the Lord for a king, God permitted Samuel to anoint Saul. By human standards, Saul met all the criteria for a leader. However, he did not have a pure heart before the Lord.

After several disappointments, God rejected Saul and sent Samuel to anoint one of the sons of Jesse as His chosen king. Once again, Samuel judged the quality of Israel's future king by outward appearance, not inner attitude and motive of heart. When at last, the youngest son of Jesse stood before him, Samuel still saw a shepherd boy, but the Lord saw his heart.

God alone can read the heart, attitudes, and motives of a person. He isn't influenced by outward show or good works. Appearances can be deceptive, but the man or woman who loves the Lord with all their heart, mind, and strength will satisfy God's heart.

As believers, we should strive to reflect Jesus. Our thoughts and minds can be influenced by either our old sin nature or new life in Christ. We may be able to fool other people, but we will never deceive the Lord. He alone knows the intent of our heart. Let us endeavor to see others through God's eyes.

Dear Lord,
Thank You for reminding me to not rely on outward appearances. Help me see others through Your eyes.

Life Interrupted
By Kathy Akins

"Let, I pray thee, thy merciful kindness be my comfort, according to thy word unto thy servant."—Psalm 119:76

THERE IS A SAYING THAT STATES, "If you live long enough, you will have to deal with change." Some changes are sneaky. As we age, our hair turns gray or leaves altogether, new wrinkles add character to our faces, and our joints stiffen with use.

There are also the dramatic changes. Those that alter our life journey and may cause us to question ourselves or even God. Life as we know it will never be the same. Sometimes we must begin again from scratch. I call these 'Life Interruptions.'

Most people will experience a life interruption several times. New jobs, health problems, marriage, children, or a loved one's death will disrupt our lives. We can adjust easily to the happy changes. But what about those causing doubt, fear, or depression? Where can you find reassurance and consolation? Only the Lord can give true comfort.

Not that long ago, I experienced a life interruption. I required back surgery, and there were unexpected complications. My hospital stay lasted two and one-half months. My dachshunds had to be fostered by friends during that time. They also experienced life interruptions.

Our journey is different now. Adaptations are being made for healing physically and mentally. My dogs seek reassurance from me through belly rubs, ear scratches, and lap time. I find my comfort with God. He provides mercy and hope. As we come through the trials of life interruptions, we can be sure of these four things:
- God keeps His promises.
- We will come through troubles with a firmer faith.
- Friends and Family may not understand all you experience, but God does.
- Our trials can be an encouragement to others.

Dear Lord,
Thank You for walking beside me and giving comfort and mercy through my life journey. May I encourage others to look toward You.

Renewal
By Stephen B. Bagley

"Jesus replied, "Very truly I tell you, no one can see the kingdom of God unless they are born again."—John 3:3

A WHILE BACK, I WAS DISCUSSING religion and life with a good friend, and he asked, "What makes Christianity so attractive to you?"

Lots of answers to that, I suspect, but for me, it may be the promise of rebirth, the promised renewal of our hearts, spirits, and lives. Not only after we're dead, although eternal life is attractive, but the possibility of new life here on this earth. Christianity says you can be reborn in this life, that you can become a new person right now. It offers change, offers a chance for us to do better, to be better.

2 Corinthians says, *"Therefore, if anyone is in Christ, the new creation has come: The old has gone, the new is here!"* This doesn't mean that your bad habits or the fallout of your bad choices magically disappear. Decisions have consequences, but it does mean that you have hope of doing better. Being reborn as a new person means you have a promise that every day offers a new chance to do better.

It sounds naïve, maybe childish, even simple, but it beats the sad sophistication and empty cynicism that we humans have elevated to an art form. Every day is the start of the rest of your life, and you have the choice to start anew. Your past does not have to define your future.

We humans make mistakes. It's comforting to know that we can be forgiven and renewed each day as we greet the morning.

Dear God,
Thank You for Your promise of rebirth. Help us embrace this gift and move forward in Your love each day.

Roll in the Grass
By Kathy Akins

"Thou wilt shew me the path of life: in thy presence is fullness of joy; at thy right hand there are pleasures for evermore."—Psalm 16:11

SEASONS IN OKLAHOMA ARE often milder than in other parts of the country. Extreme temperatures do happen, but they usually only last for days or weeks, not months, at a time. My little dachshunds like to take advantage of the weather breaks by racing to the yard. They will spend hours running, rolling, and rummaging in the grass. Pure joy.

The chaos of this world tends to draw focus away from simple pleasures. What is truly important gets crowded out by obligations and responsibilities. So much "stuff" is crammed into each twenty-four hour day that we can lose sight of living.

This is not unique to people of the twenty-first century. During Jesus' earthly ministry, many approached Him with interest in His teaching. Some refused to turn loose of their possessions and positions to follow Him. Their "stuff" blocked the view of a life full of joy with Jesus.

It is essential to spiritual health to release the clutter in our lives. Just as my dachshunds find pleasure in rolling in the grass, we may find pleasure in simple things. When we spend time in the presence of the Lord and discover the path of life He has for us, we experience the fullness of His joy.

Dear Lord,

Help me to slow down and enjoy the simple pleasures in this life. Teach me through Your Word to be who You want me to be.

Seek Good
By Wendy Blanton

"Seek good, not evil, that you may live."—Amos 5:14

I STILL REMEMBER THE FIRST TIME I really noticed this verse. It wasn't the words, so much, as the way it was formatted:

> Seek good, not evil
> That you may live

Until I saw the words stacked together in that particular Bible, I'd never realized 'evil' is 'live' backward. I'm a writer. Words are my medium. How had I not noticed that?

According to Amos, there are two choices: evil or live. When we choose good, it seems like we should get rewarded, and we will, but we're human. We want it now. We see bad things happen to good people, and our hearts weep for them. But when we see good things happen to bad people, the unfairness is a slap in the face. We can tell ourselves that life isn't fair and try to get over it, but that's easier said than done. Before you know it, evil has a toehold.

I look at it this way. I can only control me, and even that's imperfect. If I try to help someone panhandling on a corner, they may take that money and buy drugs, or they may buy food for their hungry children. What they do with the money doesn't affect me. I've tried to help a fellow human, and that's where my involvement ends. The moment they take the money from me, what they do is on them. I'll answer for my actions, and they will answer for theirs. I'm either giving them a hand or more rope to hang themselves. God sends rain on the just and the unjust (**Matthew 5:45**).

Jesus commands us to love one another as He loved us. It's often harder than it sounds. We can do only our imperfect best, and it starts by choosing good. If we seek good, not evil, we will live forever with Him.

Strength in Christ
By Kathy Akins

"And he said unto me, My grace is sufficient for thee: for my strength is made perfect in weakness. Most gladly therefore will I rather glory in my infirmities, that the power of Christ may rest upon me. Therefore I take pleasure in infirmities, in reproaches, in necessities, in persecutions, in distresses for Christ's sake: for when I am weak, then am I strong." —**2 Corinthians 12: 9-10**

GOD KNOWS OUR HEARTS. He knows the temptations we face and our tendency to sin. He knows our daily struggles with physical, emotional, and spiritual undertakings. He wants to communicate with us and help us because He loves us.

In chapter 12 of his second letter to the Corinthians, Paul shared some of his own struggles in his walk with Christ as an encouragement. This message has been a great comfort to countless believers down through the ages: "My Grace is Sufficient."

Even though Paul doesn't identify what he calls a thorn in his flesh, it pained him enough to plead with the Lord to remove it. He asked many times before the Lord answered, but not in the way that Paul wanted. Rather than remove the thorn, Paul was assured that he would be given God's grace to bear it.

Prayer is communication with God. When we are afflicted with thorns, we should pray. The Lord will always answer, but as with Paul, the answer may not be what we expect. He may not remove our troubles, but He grants us grace sufficient enough to endure them.

The grace of the Lord is enough to strengthen us, cheer our spirits, and support our souls in all afflictions. Paul was not only able to rejoice in his sufferings, but he was enabled to glorify in them as well.

What a great testimony to the grace of God! No matter what we face, there is a mightier force at work. We can boast gladly in our weakness because we are strong in the grace of Jesus Christ.

Dear Lord,
Thank You for giving me grace sufficient for all my needs. Help me rejoice in Your power, made perfect in my weakness.

The Measure of Success
By Wendy Blanton

"He has shown you, O mortal, what is good. And what does the LORD require of you? To act justly and to love mercy and to walk humbly with your God."—Micah 6:8

I WENT TO A CHRISTIAN writers' conference recently, and, as usual, it was a combination of education, inspiration, and church moments. One of the messages I was meant to hear is that God doesn't judge success by human standards. He doesn't care how much money you make or how many followers you have on Facebook®. He only cares that you love Him and are willing to carry out the plans He has for you.

What's your standard for success? Are you despondent if you're not keeping up with the Joneses? Does it ruin your day when you're passed over for promotion? Or when someone else takes credit for your work?

It's hard to see things through God's eyes. Our worldly selves cringe when we compare our circumstances to those who seem more successful. But we don't know their whole story. Only God knows that. Only God knows yours.

Take heart, Christian. God is in those things. Frank Peretti worked in a ski factory before he became a best-selling author. He has worldly success now, but he had to be humbled before that happened. God is working on all of us. We just have to listen and act, and we'll be successful.

The Tenacity of a Weed
By Wendy Blanton

"For you have need of endurance, so that when you have done the will of God you may receive what is promised." — Hebrews 10:36

I SAW A SIGN OUTSIDE A CHURCH several years ago that said, "Lord, give me the tenacity of a weed." I thought about it this morning when I moved a bag of potting soil I'd left on my patio all winter and found what I think was a prickly lettuce plant (a cousin of dandelion) that had taken root.

I knew it was there—I could see the plant, but the root system extended several inches in all directions. It was healthy despite being squashed between twenty pounds of plastic-encased dirt and concrete for several months. Its conditions didn't stop if from doing what it needed to do, and it was a fine, healthy weed until I moved the bag. I'm pretty sure it won't stay that way. If only it were that easy with all of them.

This is what I aspire to—strong and healthy with deep roots that, rather than being stopped, grow with adversity. That's easier said than done, of course. When we face a health crisis or job loss, it's easier to turn inward, to dwell on the hardship, and maybe throw ourselves a pity party. But if we try to look beyond the current circumstances, to push deeper into God's promises, we find the strength and endurance we need.

Jesus never promised life would be easy. In fact, in **John 16:33**, He said, *"I have said these things to you, that in me you may have peace. In the world, you will have tribulation. But take heart; I have overcome the world."* It doesn't get much plainer than that.

When things look dark, God's got it. When you don't know what to do, all you have to do is breathe and pray. He works all things for the good of those who believe in Him.

Sapulpa Public Library
27 W. Dewey Ave.
Sapulpa, OK 74066-3909

Even the Old Were Young Once
By Kathy Akins

AROUND THE TIME THAT I TURNED twelve years old, I became aware that my older family members had once been young. This discovery came about when my mother received a package of recent vacation photos in the mail. We lived in a small town and the only way to have personal pictures developed was to send the camera roll of film through the mail to a photo-developing company. The pictures returned the same way, along with negatives to provide the opportunity to have additional photos developed later.

I had received a simple Kodak camera as a gift on my last birthday and was fascinated with photography. Knowing that some of those photos were my handiwork, I was anxious to see how they turned out. The pictures were from our latest camping trip that included my grandparents. My grandma had worn pants for the first and only time on that trip. She never wore anything but dresses that she made herself.

I realized that I didn't know much about my grandparents as I studied those pictures. Nothing really, other than the fact that they were old, according to my twelve-year-old thoughts. I knew that my parents had once been young, because, every once in a while, they each had shared childhood experiences. But I never tied together the fact that if my parents had a life before they were my parents, then my grandparents had lived a lifetime before they were my grandparents. Mind blown! That became the summer of my awakening to the fact that my senior family members had a story to tell.

Reflecting back on my childhood, what I thought was ordinary, truly was special. Growing up a mile outside of town in a three-bedroom home on four acres gave my brother and me space to breathe, holler, and expend the energy of our imagination. My grandparents owned five acres that joined our property, and their house was a short walk across the pasture. My brother and I made the trip almost every day and had a well-worn path to show for it. My grandparent's property had an added bonus—a small pond where my brother liked to fish. He would also challenge my granddad to domino games when the weather didn't permit outdoor activity.

I could usually be found helping my granddad in the garden or searching for new kittens in his barn while he moved hay bales to make them easier to find. I also enjoyed spending time with my grandma in the kitchen as she baked cookies. She baked every day and her cookie jar was never empty.

Shortly after my realization that there was more to know about their lives, I decided to question my grandma on one of my visits. We were sitting at her kitchen table waiting on the last batch of cookies to bake when I asked, "Grandma, do you have any pictures of when you were young?"

She seemed startled by my question but replied, "A few. Pictures were harder to come by than they are now. Why?"

"I would like to know more about you before you became a grandma."

"Oh," she said just as the timer went off, telling us that the cookies were ready to come out of the oven. After transferring them to the cooling rack, Grandma disappeared into her bedroom. She was gone for several minutes, and I decided that I must have been prying into her business. That thought vanished when Grandma reappeared carrying a cardboard box. She set it on the table and I could see PICTURES handwritten across the top.

Pulling handfuls of old photographs from the box, Grandma spread them out on the table. I stared at the unfamiliar faces and wasn't sure where to begin. Black and white photos of little girls with hair in ringlets, tied with wide ribbons. They wore old-fashioned dresses with lace collars, thick tights, and uncomfortable-looking shoes. None were smiling. Other photos were of adults wearing the same style of clothing in stiff, heavy fabric. They also wore uncomfortable-looking shoes and sour expressions.

Picking up a faded photo of a girl who appeared to be around two years old, Grandma said, "This is me."

I was amazed that she actually had a picture of herself that young.

"I was the oldest child," she said. "I had five sisters and one brother. Johnny, my brother, was the youngest. He was born when I was sixteen." Grandma handed me the picture. "After I learned to sew, I helped my mother out by sewing my own clothes. By the time I was eight years old, I was making all the clothes for myself and my sisters."

My grandma sewed better than anyone I knew. She had made all of my school clothes for as long as I could remember. Now I knew that she was well practiced. She had been sewing almost her entire life. She also quilted out of necessity and taught herself crochet, knitting, and tatting, which is a technique for making lace out of thread from a series of knots and loops. To this day, I still have some of the beautiful pieces made by her hands.

We spent the rest of that afternoon looking through pictures. Every time I found one that looked especially interesting, she was able to share names, dates, and stories of the people captured by the camera. Not wanting to lose the momentum of learning family history, I begged to continue these sessions. She finally agreed that we could drag out the picture box once a week until we ran out of pictures or I got tired of looking at them. It lit a new fire in me. One that grew into a love of genealogy, particularly my genealogy.

For the remaining weeks of summer, Grandma would open her picture box and spread photos across her kitchen table. One of my favorite pictures was of my granddad standing, facing a mule that was reared up on his hind legs, with his front legs draped across my granddad's shoulders. They looked eye to eye. What struck me the most was the abundance of my granddad's dark hair. As long as I could remember, he only had a sprinkling of whitish, gray fuzz that required a straw hat to avoid sunburn when outdoors. I loved that picture. The mischievous expression reflected in his eyes was familiar. I saw it every time he moved hay bales in search of kittens or he teased my grandma. If I could have talked Grandma out of it, I would be in physical possession of that picture today, not just the memory of it.

Many of those pictures prompted detailed stories. As I learned more, I wanted to know more. I had decided that maybe boys weren't all icky and when my mother told me how she met my dad, I found it romantic and intriguing. I wanted to know how Grandma and Granddad met too.

My grandma shared the story:

Because of their large family, Grandma's dad sought work wherever he found it. By the time she was a senior in high school, class of 1921, he had his own cab. Upon graduation, Grandma wanted to attend college at Oklahoma Baptist University. Knowing that oil production activity in communities close by there was increasing, her dad decided to move the entire family to that area. He felt that his cab service would prosper and Grandma could attend the college she desired.

After a semester of college, Grandma took the exam to obtain a teaching certificate and passed with flying colors. She was hired along with another single, young woman, to teach at a two-room school east of Shawnee. The two women got along very well, until the day they met my granddad for the first time.

The school was located on a country road. The area had received a lot of rain in recent days causing the dirt road to turn muddy with deep ruts. They were in the habit of traveling alone by wagon between home and school. On their way home, the wagon slid sideways and a wheel fell into one of the deep ruts. They were stuck. While they discussed whether to walk home or try to dislodge the wheel themselves, a young man on a horse approached them. Noting their dilemma, he offered to help pull the wagon free. It took a bit of work, but he did succeed. Both women were infatuated.

When he asked to see my grandma again, of course she agreed. Unfortunately, because there seemed to be some jealousy between the women, they soon became rivals. My granddad may have enjoyed the attention, but he only had eyes for my grandma. Some months later, they married and began their life together.

I learned a lot that summer. I began to see my grandparents as people who had lived an extraordinary life. They were no longer old. They were gold.

Lessons from Chicago
By Wendy Blanton

I REMEMBER THE MOMENT, but not what day it was. I was sitting at a red light on a beautiful late-spring morning, waiting to cross Roosevelt Road from Oak Park to Berwyn, on my way home from dropping my husband off at the train station. Caffeine levels were sufficient for driving, but barely. Traffic was heavier than normal, not that there's ever really much difference in Chicago-land when people are trying to get to work. To say I was grouchy is an understatement.

I'd spent five years grumbling about what I didn't like about living there, dwelling on the negative. I longed for the day when we'd be able to leave the traffic, constant noise, fighting for parking, unpleasant neighbors, barking dog, sirens from the firehouse a block away, and the thrice daily Mommy Parades down our street to the nearby schools. I chafed at the twice a day trips to the train station two and a half miles north because bus service wasn't reliable, and parking was expensive.

We'd thought moving from the city to the suburbs would be a positive change, and it was, sort of. We'd done enough research to know Berwyn was safe, overall. If we had also checked population density, we'd have realized Berwyn is the most densely populated city in Illinois. We left Chicago for the most peopley place in the state. Ever hear God laugh at you? I did when I learned that bit of trivia. Instead of being happy, I was holding on for dear life.

The light was still red. I looked across the street to my left and saw Friendly Tap, a coffee shop by day and bar by night, just a half mile from my house. Their coffee was good, and they had a nice selection of tea. Best of all, it wasn't a national chain.

I should walk up there and work for a while, I thought. *The exercise will do me good. I do like having places like that I can walk to.*

That's when the light bulb came on. I'd miss having places like that in walking distance when we were finally able to escape Chicago.

That got me to thinking about other things I'd miss—our church, where I worked and worshipped, and the chosen family we'd built because of it. The yoga studio with multiple locations and several different classes every day. The Field Museum, where I never failed to find world-building inspiration. Endless places to walk—restaurants, coffee shops, parks. The backyard garden we'd had our friend design and build. Our quirky, almost 100-year-old bungalow. The barbecue joint we frequented, and the Chinese place across the street where I had *mushu* for the first time. Turns out, it really is a food, not just the name of the dragon in the Disney animated version of *Mulan*.

That moment, I made the shift I needed to make our remaining time bearable. As it turns out, there wasn't as much as we thought. Six months later, my husband's employer downsized. He went to work one morning, and was back before lunch. It wasn't the first time that had happened, but it was the first time we didn't have weeks of warning. A mere two months after that, we sold the bungalow and moved back to the St. Louis area, just before Christmas, and a few short months before Covid-19 shut the nation down.

In the years that have passed, we've been able to see what we really got from our sojourn in Chicago. My husband got work experience he needed for the job he has now. I learned it's good to be dependable and flexible at work, but there are limits. We grew as a couple, and our faith deepened. The time away from our children made us appreciate being near them even more than we would have if we'd never left. The population density and noise made us beyond grateful to find a house with a half-acre, neighbors nearby but with windows that don't line up with ours, and the ability to sit outside and hear birds and the wind instead of dogs and heat pumps. For the first time in our lives, we both feel like we've found our home.

Is it perfect? Not even close. But we've spent two years randomly telling each other how happy we are here. That counts for a lot.

Trapped in a Castle
By Debbie Anderson

I HAD NEVER BEEN OUT of the United States, but I always wanted to, so when I was given my first year, tax-free pass to travel anywhere my airline flew, I was ecstatic. Three of my work friends and I decided we would go overseas. We debated for days as to where we would go. There were so many options—Paris, London, Rome, Frankfurt—the list seemed endless. Finally, we chose Brussels. Yes, Brussels. One of our group once had a Belgian waffle years before when the World's Fair was in New York. She wanted to go to Belgium ever since. We agreed to go. None of us had been to any other country so we would start there.

A few weeks later we were on our way. We dressed in our most official-looking suits (a requirement in those days) and flew first class. It was amazing. We chose our meals from a menu, received warm damp towels so we could freshen up, and watched a movie for no additional charge. Plus, our seats reclined low enough we could sleep without having to sit up.

We arrived in Brussels at five-thirty in the morning. I hadn't been able to sleep so I followed the others through the routine of collecting our bags and navigating customs. Then we headed for the door. Outside there was a long line of taxis waiting for fares.

We quickly approached the one closest and told him where we wanted to go. The driver responded in Flemish. He didn't speak English. We went to the next cab, no English there either. We went through the whole line. No English. No one could help us.

There we stood on the sidewalk outside the airport entrance, surrounded by our luggage and no way to get to our hotel. We were tired and in need of a shower. We began asking other passengers if they were from Belgium and if they spoke English, hoping someone could tell the drivers where we wanted to go. Eventually, a man stopped and offered to help. After hearing we were staying at the Saint Catherine Hotel, he gave us directions assuring us it wasn't far. "When you come to an intersection stay to your left—always to the left."

So off we went navigating the streets of Brussels, staying to the left. Before long we realized we were lost. We followed his directions and should have arrived at our hotel but there was no sign of it.

We went back to asking people in the street. Most shook their heads and kept walking, some responded with *"No Anglé,"* others just passed by. Finally, we saw a nun and approached her. In broken English, she told us she was going to the St Catherine Cathedral which was next to the hotel. We walked with her to our destination.

We quickly changed and headed out to find Belgian waffles. That didn't take long since there was an open-air Belgian Waffle stand near the hotel. We all ordered the large, thick waffles, with strawberries and whipped cream. It was worth the trip. We returned for more waffles several times during our four-day visit.

At the end of the day, we decided to go to bed early and make a fresh start in the morning. We headed for the hotel bar for a celebratory drink before turning in. We all ordered a mixed drink only to be told by the bartender they didn't serve them. We could buy a glass of rum and a glass of cola, but not a rum and cola. Finally, we all agreed to order vodka and cola. Sounds strange, I know, but they didn't have rum. They also didn't believe in ice. We were served a tall glass of vodka and a tall glass of cola. The cola contained one ice cube.

"What are we supposed to do with this?" exclaimed Michelle. "Are we supposed to drink the vodka straight? I can't do that!"

The rest of the group felt the same. I suggested we sip down the vodka to where we could add cola. As we drank it down, we could add more cola. Everyone agreed in theory, but no one wanted to drink any vodka straight. Finally, I decided to take one for the team. One by one I took the glasses of vodka from my friends and drank down a few inches. The vodka was served in tall glasses that were filled to the brim, so even removing an inch or two of the liquid still left the glasses at least three-fourths full. We added soda to replace the missing vodka, then drank it down until we could add more cola. Upon finishing our drinks, we went to our rooms and slept quite well.

The next morning, we struck out to explore Brussels. It's a beautiful city with ancient architecture and narrow streets. The more modern areas featured wide avenues with newer buildings. The old and new worked together, creating a colorful, ancient, yet modern, city.

Not far from our hotel was the Grand Place, pronounced *Grande Plaz*. A large courtyard of sorts, surrounded by baroque guildhalls, with two large edifices on each end. One is the Flamboyant Town Hall (Flamboyant referring to a type of Baroque architecture, even more decorative than plain Baroque Architecture) and the neo-Gothic Kings House or Bread House. Originally, the square housed the main marketplace for Brussels. The guildhalls housed the bread store, the meat store, and the cloth store, all owned by the Duke. They were able to stay open even if the weather was bad, but more importantly, they were close by so the Duke could keep an eye on things and collect taxes. It was centrally located to the towns and villages in Belgium and France, near the causeway that ran between Flanders and the Rhineland, and was the furthest navigational point inland to reach Senne River. The market was first erected in the eleventh century.

The Town Hall was built between 1401 and 1455, transforming the square into the center of municipalities. The Duke, who was low on funds, sold many of his buildings to merchants who sold their wares in them. They built more elaborate buildings to show off their new status. The Town Hall was topped by a spire 315 feet in the air and topped by a statue of St. Michael slaying a demon.

Not to be out outdone, the Duke of Brabant erected a new building, where the cloth and bread houses had once stood across from the Town Hall. He built it in the Flamboyant style of the time and called it the Duke's House. Later to be named the King's House, when the Duke of Brabant became the King of Spain, although no king ever lived there. As the guilds and merchants grew in wealth and status, they built their houses around the Grand Place.

We spent hours exploring the shops along the Place. The King's House now is home to the Museum of Belgium, housing statues and tapestries from the 14th and 15th centuries. However, our attention was drawn to a small shop on one of the corners. The Godiva Chocolatier was a true highlight of our trip, and we visited it several times.

Entering the shop, the clerk greeted us in Flemish, but once she realized we were American, she spoke good English with a fun Flemish accent. She let us sample her wares, and it was all delicious. Offering a silver tray of various chocolates, she explained they were *meilk chocolates*. As we took a piece, we all repeated *me-ilk cho-co-lates*. They were delicious. We wanted more of this meilk chocolate. It wasn't until later we realized she was saying milk chocolate.

As we went from shop to shop, we heard of something happening that night at the Grand Place. People excitedly made plans to return. Not wanting to miss any excitement, we decided we would, too.

Returning to our hotel, we showered and prepared for our evening out. After a light meal, we strolled through the narrow streets to the area we had already visited, but it wasn't the same. The brightly lit Grand Place was alive with hundreds of people, all talking loudly to be heard. Most of the shops were closed so the activity was in the streets. We wove our way through the people, stopping from time to time, to watch a street performer. It was great fun, but not being familiar with the local nightlife, we soon thought we had experienced all there was to see. We were wrong.

"What do you think? What do you want to do now?" I asked my companions.

"Follow us," replied a voice from behind me. I turned to find a group of students from Amsterdam, who was there on a school break.

By the time I turned back to my friends, they were already following them. I joined the parade that led us to the huge King's House. The enormous wooden door looked like the entrance to a medieval castle, which it almost was. Walking in, we were led to ancient stairs leading to a cellar. I was getting nervous; after all, we didn't know these people leading us. Were we going to a dungeon? I didn't need to fear. At the bottom of the stairs was a small, crowded bar. We found a table, and one of the boys ordered a pitcher of blond beer. I had never heard of blond beer. I didn't like beer, blond or otherwise, but blond beer is just beer. Not to be confused with dark beer or ale.

We had a nice time talking to the students and comparing our stories of being American to theirs of being Dutch. I found out that even though I am half German, I do not look German. Germany is still not well-liked in Belgium or the Netherlands. Fortunately, they thought I looked Swiss, which is a part of my dad's ancestry and is looked upon fondly. Before long, the bartender announced the bar was closing.

Everyone funneled to the stairs and began their ascent to the door. There was a ladies' room about halfway up, and one of my friends needed to use the facilities, so I joined her. It didn't take long to finish our business since no one else was there, but when we opened the door to leave, we were met with complete darkness.

We couldn't see anything. Chills ran up my spine as I considered the possibilities.

What if we fell on the old stone steps? What if someone was waiting for us in the dark?

As quickly as possible, we felt our way up the stairs, walking our hands along the wall. Where had everyone gone? The place had been so crowded, and within minutes they were all gone. Even our other two friends had left us. When we got to the top, we felt better; the door was just a few feet away. Still feeling the walls as we went, we finally felt the solid wood of the massive door. Gripping the handle, I pulled, but the door didn't budge. I pushed. Nothing moved. Betty gave it a try with the same success. I heard her voice crack as she said, "I think we're trapped!"

"Don't worry. We'll get out of here, as soon as someone knows we're here." We frantically pounded on the door, but it was so gigantic, it didn't make any noise. We started yelling and pounding, knowing our voices probably weren't carrying to anyone outside.

I began to tell myself that staying overnight in an ancient castle, in total darkness was no big deal. The stone floor might not be comfortable, but we could do it. We pounded harder and yelled louder.

Surely, there hadn't been time for the people who ran the bar to finish up and leave. They had to be there, someplace, but where? How would we find them in this darkness? We'd probably fall down some stairs or knock something over if we blindly felt our way to look for them. And if they were there, why were there no lights?

We pounded and yelled louder still. Eventually, we heard some voices yelling back from the other side of the door. It was the other two friends.

"We're locked in," I called. "See if you can find help."

"Everyone's gone," they replied.

"Someone has to be around. Walk around and find someone. We're trapped!"

"I'll look, but you might have to stay there until someone comes in the morning."

Comforting.

Betty, the girl stranded with me, started to cry. I was trying to be the strong one but this place was giving me the creeps!

"We can't find anyone. We're going to go back to the hotel. Maybe the desk clerk will know what to do. If not, we'll see you in the morning." Our friends left.

I had nearly given up and found myself a place to spend the rest of the night. Betty kept asking things like, "What if there are rats?" and "What if they don't come back until time to open the bar?" She wasn't helping!

"What if we have to go the bathroom?"

I looked in the direction of her voice. "We know where the bathroom is. We even know there is a light in there. Maybe we should make our way back there for the night."

"Sleep on the floor of the bathroom? No way! I can't imagine anything grosser than sleeping on the floor of a public bathroom!"

"Not even sleeping with rats?" I asked.

I began yelling again, this time inside. I took a few steps into the darkroom and screamed, "Help! We're still here! We can't get out!"

I slid my feet a few more inches into the room. "Help us! We're trapped in here! Is there anyone here?"

Silence. My heart was pounding. Maybe it wouldn't have been so bad if we could see something. Anything. But this was before cell phones and neither Betty nor I smoked so we didn't have a lighter or even a match.

I tried one last time. "Please, help us! We can't get out! Help!"

Nothing.

I turned back to where I thought Betty was, "I think we're stuck. There's no one to help us. Do you want to sleep up here or go back to the ladies' room?"

"What are you doing here?" a voice boomed from inside the castle.

"We got locked in," I answered.

"When I say to leave, you're supposed to leave!"

"We stopped in the ladies' room. When we came out, everything was dark."

We were still in darkness. I couldn't see who this voice belonged to, but it wasn't friendly. I heard him mumbling angrily in Flemish. Then I felt him pass by and heard a key rattling.

The door opened to an empty courtyard. The people were gone. The lights were gone.

The man told us to leave, and next time we better leave when he said to leave. We assured him that next time we would hold it until we got home. We hurried past him.

I don't remember his face. I don't think I ever saw it. I do remember his tree trunk-sized arms and his massive chest. I remember thinking he was a real giant! If he would have started saying *fee-fi-fo-fum*, I would have probably died right there.

Instead, Betty and I ran all the way to the hotel. Our friends were sipping on hot chocolate in the bar. They didn't seem too worried about us. We went to the room and got ready for bed. Neither of us said much.

"I was never so scared in my life," Betty commented quietly.

"Yeah, but what a great story we have! How many people can say they were trapped in a castle?" I replied.

A Mirror, Forlorn
By D.E. Chandler

All I have to show you is yourself.
You come and stare into me daily—
gaze into my eyes, but they are yours.
Still, you stand and search for something more.

You come and stare into me daily,
As if this pure reflection's not enough.
Still you stand and search for something more—
Our face twisted in sullen self-regard.

As if this pure reflection's not enough,
though arms, and legs, and face are mirrored perfectly,
our face, twisted in sullen self-regard.
Gaze into my eyes, but they are yours.

Though arms, and legs, and face are mirrored perfectly,
You come and stare into me daily.
Gaze into my eyes but they are yours—
All I have to show you is yourself.

Carroll after Dark
By D.E. Chandler

Don't read Carroll after dark,
Doing so could leave a mark-
In the soul and on the mind;
Many fear what's left behind.

If in the dark you dare not go
For fear of darkness—don't read Poe.
For in that tiny dreaded hour,
Darkness may *your* light devour.

Mark your authors, mark them well
For Dante took us straight to Hell,
King to realms of horror deep
And Gygax to the Dragons' Keep.

Herbert birthed the spice of Dune
And Tolkien warred o'er elven rune.
Asimov coined robot law,
And Bradbury the Martians saw.

Madness is not for everyone-
And many writers are undone.
Unless you'd bear the writer's mark—
Don't read Carroll after dark.

High Maintenance
By Stephen B. Bagley

If I could somehow offer you
my heart on a silver tray
garnished with gold truffles
topped with a sprinkle of diamonds,
would it finally be enough?

Or perhaps steal for you
the sweet hymn of heaven,
which only archangels
have gloriously sung,
would you be satisfied?

Maybe even wrestle time itself
and plunder from its secret vault
the elixir of eternal youth
so age never touches your lush body,
could you be content then?

But the more important question may be
if I could do those wondrous things
if such miracles I could bring forth
as easy as buttering my bread,
why oh why would I waste them on you?

Lost
By Kathy Akins

She's not herself anymore,
forgetting simple things.

She dwells on childhood memories,
what fondness each one brings.

Each day is more confusing,
as cobwebs crowd her mind.

Dementia stole her future,
and left her body behind.

Oppenhiemer
By D.E. Chandler

A ripple skipped across the glass lake
Cool singularity in a still mind
Movement in the deep

A ripple skipped across the vast lake
All eyes widened when the earth moved in time
Commotion in the night

They peer through glasses for the countdown
Witnessed from behind leaded concrete
A ripple skipped across the dry lake

And Robert wept.

Personal Armageddon
By Stephen B. Bagley

In our personal Armageddon
no armies of glory marched.
No horned fiends with sulfur smiles
raised mailed fists against Heaven.
No Lucifer, no Michael met
with mighty thunderous blows.

The only beast, our dying love.
The only sword, our razor words.
The only flag, weary white.

Six months now have passed
since our marriage ended at Megiddo.
Today I surprised myself
by smiling at a woman I didn't know.
I guess even after Armageddon
blades of grass eventually grow.

Prodigal
By Kathy Akins

My journey was a struggle
I traveled it alone.
My burden is now lifted,
I'm finally going home.

Today my father welcomes,
his open arms I'll find.
Today we will start over,
the past left far behind.

I am no more the lost son
my father mourned for years.
My actions are forgiven
swept away by his tears.

Whispers
By Stephen B. Bagley

He whispered as he held her,
"This could get messy—
this thing between us.
We could lose everything
for a stolen moment.

"Stolen from this empty world
that breaks everything
eventually. We will break
too, you must know.

"A cross word, a sideways glance,
a silence at the wrong time.
I'll be cold, you'll be hot,
and all clocks wind down.

"Since it will end,
we walk away now.
We do the smart thing.
Protect our fragile hearts."

She whispered,
"I'm sure you're right,
but if that's so,
why then am I
still in your arms?"

He didn't reply
and held her close
as the moon sailed toward
the shores of morning.

Arda, the Dragonriders Drink
By Wendy Blanton

IF YOU KNOW ANYTHING ABOUT ME, you know I have coffee in my veins. When I started developing my fictional world, Balphrahn, I didn't want my dragon riders to be addicted to caffeine, so I developed a cocoa/chai combo called *arda*.

For my first attempt, I used ¾ cup whole milk with ¼ cup cream. The result was a rich, high-calorie, high-fat, super-filling small cup. Personally, I like to savor my hot drinks for a long time, so I switched to 2% milk for the next attempt, and it was better. I've also used almond milk, and that's my favorite so far.

A note on the spices: I mix my own chai spice using 1 part clove, 2 parts cardamom, and 4 parts cinnamon. It's not a "proper" recipe, but it's what I like. Adjust it to your taste or buy in premixed.

Arda

1 cup milk
1 ounce semisweet bakers chocolate
1/8 t chili powder
Spices:
1 cinnamon stick
1-2 cloves
  OR
½ teaspoon ground cinnamon
1/8 teaspoon clove
Optional: pinch of white pepper or a couple of white peppercorns, cardamom, ginger

Warm the milk in a saucepan with the spices and simmer for about 5 minutes. (You can infuse it longer if you want bolder flavors.) If you're using ground spices, line your strainer with a coffee filter since the spices can make the arda feel gritty.

Strain the spices out and put in the chocolate. Simmer and stir until the chocolate is completely melted.

Sweeten to taste with the sweetener of your choice. Froth with a whisk before serving.

Biscuits and Gravy
By Heath Stallcup

NOTHING SCREAMS COUNTRY MORE THAN a steaming plate of biscuits and gravy. If anybody ever tells you that biscuits and gravy isn't considered a real meal, stay away from them. You don't need that kind of negativity in your life. Besides, that just tells you that they aren't doing it right.

The best biscuits and gravy comes with a large side of bacon. Sausage is optional, but bacon, that's where it's at. The grease makes the best rue for the gravy and it adds a salty, smoky flavor to the gravy that sausage just can't provide.

Biscuits

- All-purpose flour
- Baking Powder
- Salt
- Oil
- Milk

(I don't measure and do my best guesstimate depending on how many people I'm feeding.)

Preheat the oven to 350 degrees.

Liberally flour the countertop.

Dump cups of flour (anywhere from two to five) in a large mixing bowl and a few dashes of salt. Add a gob of baking powder and mix all together. Add a medium splash of oil, then add milk while stirring with a large wooden spoon. If the mixture is too dry, you can add more milk, but it's hard to incorporate. If it's too wet, you can sprinkle more flour across the top and incorporate it much easier.

Dump the mixture onto your floured work space and use a rolling pin to roll it out, folding it over a few times and pressing it back flat. This adds 'layers' to your biscuits so you can separate them later.

You can use a biscuit cutter or a straight edged glass to punch them out. Drop the discs onto loose flour then place them in the pan. You can set the biscuits next to each other, but they'll cook faster and more evenly if you can leave a bit of air space around them.

Bake for about 20 minutes or until the tops are a nice golden brown. This cooking time can vary depending on the amount of moisture in your dough, the types of flour, and the ambient temperature.

Gravy

While the biscuits are baking, you'll have plenty of time to make gravy. Use a slotted spatula as it helps to prevent lumps.

You'll want the grease at about medium temp. Sprinkle flour into your bacon grease. (Oil will NOT work. You need a fat that is a solid at room temperature in order to make good gravy.) Mix thoroughly with your slotted spatula. You don't want your rue to get too thick, or you risk lumps. How much grease do you start with? We have a large family. I usually cook up about three pounds of bacon at a feeding and will use anywhere from a third to half of the grease left over for gravy. The rest goes into a Mason jar for other foods like fried taters.

Once your flour is thoroughly incorporated, turn the heat to high. You want to brown the rue a bit, and it helps to remove a lot of the starchy flavors from the gravy. Once it comes to temperature, I usually add spices. Salt and pepper to your taste (garlic powder optional, but my kids love it). Stir the spices into the rue, then pour your milk. For our family, it's about a half gallon of whole milk.

As soon as you've poured the milk, increase the temperature to HIGH and stir with the spatula, ensuring that you scrape the bottom of the frying pan. Try to keep the entire bottom of the pan scraped as you stir. This will prevent your gravy from scorching, and it removes a lot of the residue from frying the bacon. Remember that you're scraping flavorful goodness from the bottom. You don't have to be super aggressive in your scraping because some won't come loose.

When the gravy starts to thicken, keep an eye on it. Some people prefer thinner gravy, others like it so thick it has to be sliced. When the gravy is ALMOST to the desired thickness, pull it from the heat and dump into a bowl. It will thicken as it cools.

Optional: Some folks like sausage gravy. If this is you, fry up sausage beforehand and dump it into your gravy bowl. Most sausages these days have little grease left over afterward, but save what you can for your rue. You'll probably need to add to it from either your bacon grease collection or use part of a stick of real butter. Pour your finished gravy over the sausage crumbles and stir it together.

Chicken and Dumplings
By Heath Stallcup

AS A KID, I HATED CHICKEN and dumplings. Not just because it reminded me of a bowl of lumpy snot, but because I was the one that had to butcher the chicken or rooster that went in the pot.

I will say this, I'd much rather have to butcher for dumplings than for the fryer. Fried chicken kept its skin which meant hours or plucking, dunking in steaming hot water and plucking some more. Then you had to scorch the skin to get those little pin feathers that might have been missed. The smells were enough that I hated eating chicken for decades afterward.

Ah, the joys of farm living.

But the odds are you already got some chicken in the freezer anyway. So let's skip to that part.

Chicken and Dumplings

Chicken meat. Can be whole or skinless, boneless

Flavorings: Salt, pepper, parsley flakes, garlic powder, dehydrated onion bits, chicken broth, Wyler's chicken flavored cubes.

Optional: Sliced celery, diced carrots, peas

Dumplings: All purpose flour, salt, baking powder, vegetable oil, milk

Bring a big pot of water to a boil and add chicken. You can salt it if you like. A lot of folks like to use the same boiling water to cook the dumplings. I prefer to replace the water once the meat is shredded. However, any seasonings you put in the initial pot will only add to the flavor of the chicken. Feel free to spice it up. If you prefer your dishes with a bit more kick, put a few pinches of cayenne in it or maybe some red pepper flakes. Garlic and onion are always good, too.

How much chicken depends on how many people, how far you want to stretch that meat out and how 'meat dense' you want the dish. You can probably get away with feeding a family of three with a single chicken breast if you wanted it to be mostly dumplings. Or you can boil up a whole chicken for one person and freeze your leftovers.

Let that chicken boil for a good long time. You want it to peel off the bone easily. If you started with skinless, boneless chicken, you still want to let it boil long enough that it easily shreds. I usually get it to an angry boil, put the lid on it, drop the heat to low and let it simmer for a couple of hours.

Strain out the water and shred that chicken up. I've cheated a time or two when time was of the essence. I took semi-frozen chicken breasts, sliced them into cubes and boiled from there.

Chicken and dumplings is one of those dishes that you can dress up as much as you like, or you can leave plain. I like to add sliced celery, carrots and frozen peas to mine just before the final boil and adding the dumplings. Yes, it adds a bit of flavor but also lots of color. I also season mine up with dehydrated onion bits, garlic powder, salt, pepper and parsley flakes. The parsley and vegetables give a nice splash of color to an bland looking dish.

Once you have shredded your chicken, bring your water to an angry boil. Feel free to add chicken broth and/or Wyler's chicken cubes to the water for added flavor. Add your seasonings and dump spoonfuls of biscuit dough into the boiling water. Try to dump the following lumps away from the last to prevent them from sticking together.

Here's a tip when it comes to dumplings…mix up as much as you think you and yours could possibly ever eat, then DOUBLE it. Trust me. If you don't, you'll swear to do it next time.

Homemade dough can be made a bit wetter than you would use to make biscuits as it doesn't need to be rolled out.

For those who haven't memorized how to make biscuits yet, you will need all purpose flour, baking powder, salt, oil and milk.

Dump a big gob of flour in a large mixing bowl, add salt to taste, and a smidge of baking powder. Mix with a whisk then add a splash of oil. Pour milk while mixing with a large wooden spoon. Mix thoroughly. Scoop up a large gob of dough and use a smaller spoon to goop off smaller lumps to drop in the boiling water. Drop the dumplings in a crisscross pattern to prevent sticking.

Resist the urge to stir the pot as it prevents your dumplings from fluffing and they'll break apart and turn into a thick goo.

Once the last of the dumplings have been spooned into the pot, lower the heat, put a lid loosely over the top, and let them cook for about twenty minutes.

Scoop it into a bowl and season to taste. I almost always put salt, pepper, garlic powder, and sometimes onion powder on mine.

Chocolate Bonbons
By Joanne Verbridge

THIS IS A GREAT RECIPE for all those family Christmas get-togethers! You'll always take home an empty dish so you might want to make a batch just for you.

Chocolate Bonbons

1 ½ box powdered sugar
1 cup margarine
½ cup chopped nuts
1 box coconut
1 can Eagle Brand Condensed Milk
3 packages of small chocolate chips
½ bar paraffin wax

Mix all ingredients except chocolate and wax. Chill mixture until mostly firm. Roll into small balls. Chill again.

Melt chocolate and wax in double boiler. Dip balls into chocolate mix, and then roll in nuts. Place balls on wax paper. Refrigerate until firm.

Chocolate Crinkles
By Joanne Verbridge

THESE BROWNIE-LIKE COOKIES 'CRINKLE' on the top due to the powdered sugar. They're perfect to serve with a scoop of vanilla ice cream!

Chocolate Crinkles

½ cup vegetable oil
4 squares melted unsweetened chocolate
2 cups granulated sugar
4 eggs
2 teaspoons vanilla
2 cups flour
2 teaspoons baking powder
½ teaspoon salt
1 cup powdered sugar

Mix oil, melted chocolate, and sugar. Blend in one egg at a time and mix well. Add vanilla. Sift flour, baking powder, and salt together. Add a little at a time to the liquid mixture. Chill several hours or overnight.

Heat oven to 350. Drop teaspoons of dough into powdered sugar and roll. Shape into balls. Placed on greased cookie sheet. Bake 10-12 minutes. DO NOT OVERBAKE!

Cordon Bleu Roll-ups
By Debbie Anderson

SHORTLY AFTER GRADUATING FROM HIGH SCHOOL, I was introduced to Chicken Cordon Bleu.

Put simply, it is a chicken breast stuffed with ham and cheese, breaded and fried. It was a favorite of mine but also a mystery. How could someone stuff a chicken breast with ham and cheese? Sounded complicated and time-consuming so I decided to let the French keep their secret. I didn't think about it again for many years.

One day, while flipping through a cookbook, I found the blue-ribbon recipe. It wasn't hard to make but it was time-consuming. I suppose it wouldn't take so long if I made a habit of making it more than once. The recipe was thrown in the recipe box, never to see the light of day again.

Now, as an adult of a certain age, I have to watch my weight. I eat a lot of chicken. I became so burned out with my usual ways to prepare this bird that I considered becoming a vegetarian. I admit I didn't consider it for long, a few seconds or so. I longed for crispy fried chicken. The kind my grandmother made. Breaded with flour and fried in Crisco®. The good kind of my youth. It was time to find an easy solution for boring chicken.

One evening, as I stared at a raw chicken breast, I remembered the Chicken Cordon Bleu of my youth. There had to be an easy way to recreate this deliciousness without blowing my diet.

I checked my refrigerator. To my surprise, I had sliced ham, and Swiss cheese. But how could I get that crispy fried coating without using flour or oil? And how could I get the ham and cheese stuffed in the chicken breast without taking all day?

It came to me as a vision—okay that's not exactly true. It was just an idea, but what did I have to lose? I would simply roll the chicken around the gooey center. Instead of flour for breading, I would use a combination of breadcrumbs and parmesan cheese, and instead of frying, I would simply bake it.

My experiment was a success. It's easy, fast, and tasty, while still being healthy.

Hope you like it.

Cordon Bleu Rollups

½ cup shredded Parmesan cheese
1/3 cup whole wheat breadcrumbs
½ teaspoon dried oregano
¼ teaspoon garlic powder
8 (2 oz) boneless, skinless chicken breast cutlets
2 tablespoons olive oil
4 (1 oz) slices of low-sodium ham
¾ cup shredded Swiss cheese
2 tablespoon chopped parsley

Place a rimmed baking sheet in the oven and preheat to 500°. (Do not remove the baking sheet while the oven preheats.)

Place parmesan cheese and breadcrumbs in a shallow bowl. Add oregano and garlic powder.

Brush cutlets with oil; dredge in breadcrumb/Parmesan mixture.

Top each cutlet with 1 piece of ham and 1 ½ tablespoon of Swiss cheese

Carefully roll cutlets, starting at the short end, secure with wooden toothpicks.

Place a sheet of parchment paper on the baking sheet, or spray with cooking spray.

Place roll-ups, seam side down, on preheated baking sheet. Bake in preheated oven for 10 minutes or until a meat thermometer inserted in the thickest portion reads 165°.

Sprinkle with parsley.

Note: Preheating the pan with the oven allows the breadcrumbs to get crispy while the chicken cooks. Remove the toothpicks before serving. Serve with a green salad. Serves four.

Depression Buttermilk Biscuits
By Joanne Verbridge

DURING THE GREAT DEPRESSION, biscuits were cheaper to make and afford than bread. In Appalachia, where this recipe is thought to have originated, the biscuits are called 'cathead biscuits.'

Ingredients

3 teaspoons baking powder
1 teaspoon salt
1 cup full fat buttermilk
Flour
Cooking oil

In a bowl, mix baking powder and salt. Add buttermilk and mix well. Allow to stand until foamy. Stir in flour until dough is easy to handle. Heat baking dish with enough oil to coat both sides of dough.

Roll dough on lightly floured board. Knead dough and roll out ¼ inch thick. Cut with cookie cutter. Coat each side of dough with hot oil. Bake until golden brown and enjoy!

Italian Beef Sandwiches
By Debbie Anderson

AS A CHILD, MY DAUGHTER, JANIE, hated anything involving the kitchen. She'd rather clean the bathroom than wash dishes. She found excuses not to learn to cook. Once we had company over for dinner. While I took the meat from the oven, I asked her to make a salad. The vegetables were already cleaned and chopped. All she had to do is tear the lettuce into a bowl and add the carrots, celery, and tomatoes.

"I don't know how to make a salad," she said.

"Janie, tear the lettuce and add the vegetables." I gave her a bowl.

"I don't know how."

I looked at this junior high-aged girl, incredulously. "Then it's time you learned."

My childless friend overheard our discussion and came to her rescue. "You can't assume a kid knows something if you haven't taught her," he scolded. "Come on, Janie, I'll show you how."

Janie watched as he pulled the bag of vegetables from the refrigerator. "I'll be right back. I need to use the bathroom."

She didn't return. Scott made the salad.

In high school, all the girls on the drill team made cookies for the football team on game day. The night before, she told me she needed cookies. I was heading for bed. "You're going to have to bake them yourself. It's not hard. Read the directions."

"I can't!"

"Then we'll leave early tomorrow and pick some up at the store."

"They have to be homemade!"

"I don't know what to tell you. Make them yourself or we buy them tomorrow. I'm going to bed."

The next morning, Janie carried a large container of homemade cookies to school. "I knew you could do it. I'm proud of you."

"Josh baked them for me."

I looked at my son, "Why?"

"She said she didn't know how. She was going to cry."

One day, I forgot to take the chicken out of the freezer before going to work. Janie, a recent high school graduate, was home so I called her and asked her to do the task. She assured me she'd take care of it. A few hours later, my boss said he was calling a meeting for the end of the day. I wouldn't be home until around eight o'clock.

I called Janie and told her the news. She would have to fix dinner for herself and her brothers. I assured her I'd call her around five o'clock and tell her what to do. Roasted chicken is not complicated.

When I called to give her instructions, she told me she forgot to take the chicken out of the freezer. I rolled my eyes and did a mental inventory of what she could make instead. "No problem," I told her. "There is a package of soup mix in the cabinet. All you have to do is put it in a pan and add water." I had her find the soup mix and look over the directions to see if there was anything she didn't understand.

"I guess I can do it," she huffed.

"The Jiffy corn muffin mix is right beside the soup mix. You just have to add an egg and milk. Think you can make that? Do you want me to wait while you read the directions?"

"No."

"Okay, you make dinner and go ahead and eat."

Later that night, I arrived home to the aroma of soup. It smelled delicious. Janie was talking on the phone. I went to the stove and lifted the lid. The soup was bubbling.

Dinner had not been served.

"Janie, why didn't anyone eat?"

"The cornbread still isn't done."

I opened the oven and found a large casserole dish with what looked like cornbread batter covered in an inch of a clear liquid. "What's this?"

"The cornbread. I told you it wasn't done."

"What's on the top of it?"

"The oil."

"That's oil? Why did you put so much oil in it?"

"That's what the recipe said to do."

"It may need a quarter cup of oil, but this is more than that!"

"I couldn't find the mix you were talking about, so I used the recipe on this."

She placed a bag of cornmeal in front of me and pointed to the recipe. I read through the ingredients. It called for ¼ cup of oil. "Janie, it says ¼ cup of oil.

"No, it says, to pour at least one inch of oil in the pan. That's step one! It's right there on the bag." She was still on the phone and was tired of the whole subject.

I read the recipe again. Then I turned the bag. On the side was a recipe for hush puppies. It did begin with pouring an inch of oil into a skillet (for frying!). She had followed step one for hush puppies, then went back to the bag and continued with the cornbread directions!

I wondered how she would feed herself when she left home. I shouldn't have worried. Once she called me and said she bought a roast and wondered what to do next. She learned. Soon she was making spaghetti. I think she kind of likes to cook now.

On a Christmas visit, I watched her put ingredients for Italian Beef Sandwiches in the Crockpot before we went to visit my parents. When we were ready to go home, she invited her grandparents to join us for dinner. Italian Beef is a specialty in the Chicago area, where she lives. The sandwiches were delicious. This time, I asked her for the recipe.

Italian Beef Sandwiches

1 small to medium beef roast (about 2lbs.)
1 small onion, chopped
1 cup of water
1 package of dry Italian Salad Dressing Mix
Sub sandwich rolls or any rolls that are fairly dense
Swiss Cheese (optional)

Cut the roast into 1-inch chunks. Place in the crock pot. Add the onions and the water. Sprinkle the salad dressing mix over top. Cover with the lid and cook on low about 5 hours or high for 3 hours.

Use two forks to shred the cooked beef. Place the beef on the buns and spoon the *au jus* over the sandwich.

If you want to add cheese, place a slice over the meat and pop it under the broiler until melted. Enjoy!

No Salt, Please!
By Debbie Anderson

MY HUSBAND WAS A TYPE-ONE DIABETIC. As soon as we were married, I made an appointment for him to see an endocrinologist. The doctor took a blood test, asked a lot of questions, and discovered Ray hadn't been to a doctor in eight years. He immediately checked him into the hospital to get his blood sugar regulated as well as instruct him on the correct way to take care of himself. That meant I needed to learn how to take care of him. After two weeks, Ray came home with a schedule of when to check his blood and a list of foods to eat and not eat. He had to eat at specific times and keep a log of his blood sugar readings and food intake. I would make sure he complied.

Salt was not included. The doctor encouraged me to cook with herbs and spices to avoid adding salt. I knew excess salt wasn't good for anyone, but food can be bland without it. I enjoy cooking and experimenting with seasonings so I took up the challenge.

I started making my own salt-free seasoned salt. I used it to cook and kept a saltshaker of it on the table. My children (from my first marriage) were two years old at the time. Being the little copycats they were, they felt they needed to 'salt' their food, too. I began sprinkling the seasoned salt on their mac-and-cheese, and they loved it. They would continue to use it until they left home many years later.

I babysat for my best friend's little girl who was the same age as my youngest. Many later, I saw her at a party. She remembered I introduced her to chocolate-chip cookies, but what she remembered the most was the salt-free seasoned salt she used to season her macaroni.

Salt-Free Seasoned Salt

4 teaspoons onion powder
3 teaspoons garlic powder
2 teaspoons paprika
3 teaspoons pepper

Mix all ingredients together. I put mine in an old saltshaker. Be sure to use onion and garlic powder, NOT onion and garlic salt.

Mole Hunt
By Kathy Akins

DAN BENTLEY SURVEYED HIS BACKYARD where multiple small mounds of dirt scattered the freshly mowed landscape. Checking his wife's flowerbeds, he could see wilted plants that had boasted healthy blooms just two days before.

"Moles," he said. "Dadburn moles are taking over the whole place." Disgusted, he walked to the patio and found an empty lawn chair in the shade. Pulling his cell phone from his pocket, he called Tom Stephens.

"Hello, Tom. This is Dan Bentley. I seem to have a mole problem. Think you can bring your dog out and have a look?"

"Sure Dan, I can be there in about an hour." Ending the call, Tom said goodbye to his companions and headed home to get Blackie.

Tom spent his mornings in the local coffee shop bragging about his dog, Blackie, the greatest mole-hunter in the country. Discovering Blackie curled up by his mailbox three years earlier, Tom had both pity for the pup and fury for the person who dumped him. An instant bond formed between man and dog.

The young cur grew fast. His legs stretched quicker than he filled out, even though he ate non-stop. By the time he finished growing, he stood two-foot tall at the shoulder and weighed around fifty pounds.

Realizing the dog's propensity for catching moles, Tom decided to put that talent to good use and advertised Blackie as a mole hunter. Soon he had built a small business. Every time someone requested Blackie's expertise, Tom had a new adventure story to share with his coffee-drinking buddies.

Dan waited on his front porch until a twenty-year-old, rusty pickup pulled into the driveway. Tom waved from the driver's side as the vehicle rolled to a stop. Stepping off of the porch, Dan returned the wave.

Dressed in striped overalls and blue work shirt, Tom crawled out of the truck. He had a habit of hooking his thumbs under the straps of his overalls when he was about to say something profound. He already had his thumbs in place by the time Dan reached him.

"Got a mole problem, huh?"

"Yeah," Dan said. "Backyard is full of 'em. Wife's not happy about her flowers either. Come take a look."

The two men walked around the side of the house to find more molehills than Dan had seen earlier.

"Yup, you got a definite problem, Dan. Nothin' for a good mole catcher like Blackie, though. He'll make short work of it. He's already excited. I think he could smell 'em when we pulled up."

They returned to the driveway.

Tom faced Dan. "I charge three dollars a mole."

"Agreed," Dan said.

Tom unloaded Blackie from the truck and walked him around to the backyard. The dog lifted his nose in the air and sniffed.

Tom unclipped the leash. "Get 'em, Blackie."

Blackie's head dove to the ground. The dog zigzagged across the yard. He stopped a few feet from where the men stood, and dug into a soft mound of dirt. Within thirty seconds, Blackie's head disappeared into the ground. He came up for air and more dirt started flying. When half of his body disappeared, he looked like one of the fake dog rump signs that decorate yards, except Blackie's rump was moving. He came up for air again.

"Time to move on, Blackie," Tom commanded.

Blackie did not show any sign of hearing his master, but moved to the next molehill where he repeated the digging process. This interaction continued at each molehill until the twenty-first hill.

Blackie's body was halfway buried in the ground when he started twitching. Scrambling backwards, his howling could be heard before his head popped out of the ground. He was slinging dirt and turning circles as soon as he was free of the hole. A mole clung to the right side of his muzzle and swung from side to side as Blackie twisted his head in an effort to break the critter's hold. Not able to shake the mole's grip, Blackie charged around the yard, alternating between howls and whines.

When the dog ran by him, Tom grabbed Blackie, plucked the mole up in one quick movement, and threw it to the ground.

While it lay stunned, Dan picked up a large stick and finished it off.

"Good boy, Blackie. You did real good." Soothing the panicked dog, Tom removed a small tube of ointment from his bib pocket, then squatted down by the whimpering pup and dabbed at the bite.

"Dan," said Tom, "I think that one mole was responsible for all your damage. One can make a lot of tunnels and a lot of hills. Your problem should be solved. That'll be three dollars."

"What?"

"We agreed to three dollars for each mole caught. Blackie caught one. That's three dollars."

"It looked more like the mole caught Blackie," Dan replied.

"Well," Tom stood and hooked his thumbs under his overall straps. "There was no mention of how Blackie would catch them. Sometimes he gets a little creative just to liven things up. Fact is he caught the mole."

Dan glanced down at Blackie who gazed back at him with liquid, brown eyes. Dan sighed. "Maybe the hunting didn't go according to plan, but you're right. The mole was caught." He pulled three one-dollar bills from his pocket and handed them to Tom, then stretched out his right hand for a handshake.

"Thanks for the help ridding my yard of vermin, Tom. Blackie is one fine mole hunter."

Tom grinned broadly as he accepted the money and the handshake. "Yup. Call if you need us again. Me 'n Blackie are always ready."

Tom scanned the yard once more. "Now that your mole problem is taken care of, your next move is filling in those holes. My cousin, Sam, over in Cedarville has a crazy ol' hound that buries everything he can find. He could make fast work of it for a reasonable price. Want me to give him a call?"

"No. Appreciate it, Tom, but I think I can take it from here."

"Suit yourself. Let's go, Blackie." Tom turned to go. He and Blackie walked back to the pickup and drove off.

Dan ambled to the garage to retrieve his shovel. He chuckled and shook his head. "Can't wait to see what story Tom will concoct out of this. Without doubt, Blackie will come out the hero. After all, he is the greatest mole-hunter in the country."

Rapunzel: A Love Story
By Debbie Anderson

ONCE UPON A TIME, in a land not so far away, a young girl named Rapunzel, lived with her parents. They, like most middle-class folks worked hard to make a living and provide her with the basics—food, clothing, and a roof over her head. Most of all they loved their little girl with all their hearts. Rapunzel was very happy.

As she grew, her parents noticed people looking at her. She was quite beautiful. Her eyes were the color of the sky on a summer day, her cheeks were rosy, and her lips were full. Her smile lit up the room. But her hair was her glory—the color of a shock of wheat blowing in the field, the shine like that of the sun. It was thick and strong. Rapunzel wore her hair to the middle of her back—long and glossy, and just right for wearing in a ponytail. Her father knew he would have to watch out for her because she was so lovely.

One day, as she walked to school with her friends, a large black car pulled up next to her. Inside sat a strange-looking little man. He had bushy gray hair and thick eyebrows that met. Slowly he rolled down the window. "Excuse me miss. Can you tell me how to get to the mall?"

"Oh yes," replied Rapunzel. She walked to his car to give him directions. As she did, the man opened his door and stepped out. Rapunzel stopped not sure what he was doing.

"Come ahead, dear," he said and smiled. "I just needed to stand for a minute. These old knees are giving me trouble."

Rapunzel, who was very young and trusting, felt instantly sorry for the man. She hurried closer so she could help him. Unfortunately for the girl, the man did not have bad knees at all. It was a trick to get her close enough to catch her. And so he did. Quick as a wink, he grabbed her and threw her in his car. Before Rapunzel knew what was happening, the car sped down the road with her in it. She screamed and tried to open her door but it was locked tight.

"Don't get so upset," said the man. "I'm going to take good care of you. You'll be my little girl now."

"But I don't want to be your little girl. I want my mommy and daddy!" Tears streamed down her face. "Where are you taking me? I want to go home!"

"You live with me now. You will have all the things a pretty girl like you will ever want. I'm your new daddy!"

"No!" shouted Rapunzel. "I don't want a new daddy. I want my daddy!" Again, she jerked on the door handle. "Let me out! Let me out!"

Suddenly, Rapunzel felt a sharp slap across the face.

"Shut up!" shouted the man. "I will not condone this intolerable screaming. If you don't stop now, I will slap you again."

Rapunzel wanted to scream even louder but decided against it since her cheek still stung from the last time. She gulped some air and tried to breathe slowly to calm herself. "Why? Why did you take me? Are you going to hurt me?"

"Hurt you? No, of course not. I get very lonely living alone in my big house. When I saw you and your beauty, I knew you were the one meant to live with me."

The girl looked at the ugly man and felt sorry for him. "I'm sorry you're so lonely. Don't you have a wife or children?"

"No," said the man. "I never found a wife and have never had children."

"Do you have a dog or a cat?"

"No, no dog or cat."

"Do you have a bird, or a turtle, or a hamster?"

"No, no birds, turtles, or hamsters. No family. No pets," he said matter-of-factly. "But now I have you. You will be my family. I won't be lonely anymore."

Rapunzel thought about this. She felt sorry that he didn't have anyone to love him. Maybe it would be alright for a little while. She could spend one night and then tomorrow when he sent her to school she would go home.

"What should I call you?" she asked.

"You could call me daddy."

"Oh no. I could never do that. I already have a daddy."

"Uncle?"

She shook her head.

"I guess you'll have to call me Gus," the man stated.

"Gus?"

"Yes, that's my name. Gus Muttly Troll."

"Gus Muttly Troll? That's an odd name."

"Yes, Gus after my father, Muttly because I was an ugly baby, and Troll because, well, because it's my last name."

Rapunzel nodded. "Okay, Gus it is. So, Gus where do you live. We've driven a long way."

"We're almost there. It's a special house with a special tower just for you."

"A tower? I've never heard of a house with a tower. Is it very tall?"

"Look for yourself." Gus pulled into a long driveway that led to a huge castle. On one side, was a tall tower several stories high with a small window at the top.

Rapunzel gasped as they parked in front of the castle. It was certainly bigger than any house in her neighborhood. Gus opened her door and let her out of the car but kept a firm hand on her shoulder until they were inside.

The entryway revealed marble floors, a polished staircase, and a chandelier that sparkled like diamonds as it hung from the ceiling several floors above them. Their steps echoed as Rapunzel followed Gus through the elegant rooms. The walls were covered with portraits of unknown people. Some had a resemblance to Gus. As they reached the dining room Rapunzel stopped and stared at the long wooden table. Twenty chairs sat on each side, not counting the two at each end. She wondered who used those chairs since Gus didn't have a family. The room although beautifully decorated, seemed cold. It was too big and empty.

"I bet you're hungry after our trip," said Gus. "I'll tell the cook to prepare our lunch."

"Cook? You have a cook?"

"Of course, how else would I be able to eat?"

Gus pulled a long, velvet cord, and soon an old woman dressed in a uniform and apron appeared.

"We're ready for lunch," Gus stated without looking at the woman.

"Who is this?" asked the cook.

"None of your business!" snapped Gus.

"I'm Rapunzel."

"I'm happy to meet you, Rapunzel," said the cook, offering her hand to the girl.

"You can call me Cook. What brings you here?"

"I said it's none of your business! Go get my lunch," snapped Gus.

The cook rushed out of the room.

"Why were you so rude to her?" asked Rapunzel.

"Who me? I wasn't rude."

"Yes, you were."

Gus's neck turned red. "I said I wasn't and that's the end of it!" he yelled. "You might as well learn now that I'm in charge here. What I say goes. There will be no arguing about it."

"That's not fair!" shouted Rapunzel, stomping her feet. She crossed her arms and glared at this man. *No wonder he doesn't have a wife or family! He's mean.*

"That's enough! There will be no lunch for you, little lady. Go to your room! Now!"

"Gladly!" Rapunzel stood to stomp off but stopped realizing she didn't know where her room was. "Where is it?"

Gus took her by the arm and led her up at least 100 stairs. When he finally stopped and opened the door, Rapunzel was startled at the beautifully decorated room.

She walked around the room, exploring every crevice, from the large, canopied bed, to the gleaming chest of drawers, and the lace-skirted vanity table crowned with an exquisite glass framed mirror. Everything sparkled. The comforter was a soft pink, the pillows were filled with feathers and the canopy, covered with pink satin, rich with embroidery and jewels, draped softly to the floor.

When she turned to thank Gus for such a wonderful room, he was gone. She went to the door but found it was locked from the outside.

Rapunzel realized she was trapped. When he let her out, she would run away. She didn't know where she was. They had driven a long way. But if she could make it to the road, someone would help her.

She opened the window and looked out upon the huge estate. There were no other houses for miles. Her screams for help would not be heard. Her stomach growled as she climbed up on the bed. How did she get here? How would she get away?

***

Years went by and Rapunzel remained trapped in her room in the top of the tower. Gus would come to her room to eat supper and discuss his day. Mesmerized by her beauty, he brought her nice clothes and jewels. He made sure she had a television, but not a phone. She could not have a computer, but she had a radio. He brought her books so she could read and allowed Cook to teach her to embroider and paint. He even brought her a guitar and she taught herself to play it.

Rapunzel gave up the notion of ever getting out of this room. She filled the hours staying busy and often found herself sitting by the window, feeling the breeze on her face and listening to the birds. She began playing her guitar and singing along with them.

Gus boarded up the doors to make sure she couldn't escape. Cook also became his prisoner. She was sure he'd lost his mind and she tried to avoid him as much as possible.

Rapunzel's hair grew quite long, reaching yards past her feet. Gus wouldn't allow her to cut it. To him, it was like spun gold and every bit as valuable. She wore it wrapped around her head to keep from stepping on it. She begged him to let her cut it and he refused. Instead, he found another use for it.

Since he boarded up the doors, he could not use them. He climbed the many stairs to Rapunzel's room each morning and had her lower her golden locks from the window. Then he would hold on to it as he slowly shimmied to the ground. At night when he returned, he would call, "Rapunzel, Rapunzel, let down your long hair." She would lower the golden strands once again and he would climb up to her window.

This was extremely painful for Rapunzel, and she often had headaches as a result. She lost all hope of ever going home. She quit eating. She stopped embroidering. The only thing she ever did was sit by the window, play her guitar, and sing sad songs along with the radio. The birds listened to her now. If birds could cry, they surely would have, for the songs were filled with such sorrow.

One day, as Rapunzel sat by her window singing, a UPS van drove up the long driveway. Lost in her sorrow, she didn't hear him arrive.

"Hey lady!" he called up to her window.

Startled, Rapunzel looked down at the handsome man in uniform. "Yes?"

"I have a package for a Mr. Joseph Lawson. Does he live here?"

"No, he doesn't."

"I didn't think anyone lived here. I noticed the door was boarded up."

"Yes," sighed Rapunzel. "Mr. Troll boarded it up so I couldn't get out."

"Seriously?"

"Yes, he's kept me captive here for many years."

"How does he get in?"

Rapunzel bowed her head embarrassed. "He climbs up my hair."

"What? How does he do that?"

She tossed her hair out the window. The ends landed at the UPS man's feet. He shook his head and scratched his chin.

"Doesn't it hurt?"

"Yes, but I'm used to it. Would you like to come up?"

"I'm not going to climb up your hair. Would you like to get out of there?"

"Yes! But he'll be back soon."

"Then I'll come back tomorrow." Rapunzel and the UPS man made arrangements for him to rescue her the next day after Gus left.

"I better go before he comes back. I still need to deliver this package."

Rapunzel watched as he made his way back to his van. "By the way," she called. "What's your name?"

"Bob, Bob Prince-Charming." He called back.

"Thank you, Bob! I look forward to seeing you tomorrow."

Bob cut a rose from a nearby rosebush and tossed it to the beautiful girl in the window. She caught it, pricking herself with a thorn. She quickly stuck her finger in her mouth to stop the bleeding. This simple gesture sent a mixture of emotions through Bob the UPS guy's heart.

"I think I love you!" he called.

"I think I love you, too!" she called back.

***

The next morning, Bob was up at dawn preparing his strategy to rescue his damsel in distress. How could anyone hold a person captive for years? Is anyone looking for her? He would be there, her knight in shining armor.

Meanwhile, Rapunzel rolled her hair up, hopefully for the last time, after Gus climbed down. All she could think about was leaving this room that had been her jail for so long. She wondered if her parents were still looking for her. A tear slid down her cheek at the thought of seeing them again. What would her life be like? Would she go back to school? Could she fit in the little desks if she did?

So much ahead of her was a mystery she was ready to take on. Most of all, she wanted to get to know Bob Prince-Charming, the UPS man who was coming for her. She thought of his rugged good looks and his kind eyes, and wondered what other types of packages he might be carrying. A strange flutter in her midsection let her know this was something new and special. She waited by the window, singing joyful songs with the birds.

Shortly before noon, she saw the UPS van approaching. Her heart beat rapidly against her chest. Then she noticed a fire truck following Bob up the drive. It was followed by two police cars.

For a moment she was afraid the house may be on fire, then she saw the long ladder on the top. They were going to save her.

"Are you ready to go?" called Bob.

"Yes! Oh, yes!" called Rapunzel.

The fireman let Bob ride in the basket as they raised the ladder to the window. He quickly helped her out of the window, then took her into his strong arms making her feel safe. As the ladder was slowly lowered, she told Bob that Cook was also trapped in the castle.

Soon, firemen were using axes to break down the doors and rescue Cook. She was so happy to finally get out that she grabbed the first fireman she could and kissed him.

Policemen checked the castle to make sure Gus wasn't hiding, even though Rapunzel told them he wasn't home. The officers called in an all-points bulletin with a description of Gus and his car. They were sure they'd find him soon, now that they knew who they were looking for. Rapunzel wasn't so sure. He'd remained free for many years after kidnapping her.

Finally, they were ready to leave. Crime scene tape crisscrossed the door. Cook rode in a police car, thrilled that they used the siren. The fireman tapped their helmets in salute as they sped off. Then it was just Bob and Rapunzel.

"Where to?" he asked. "Want to go see your parents? I'm sure they'll be thrilled to know you're alright."

"I want to see them, but later."

"Okay. Where do you want to go?"

"Can you take me to Super Cuts? I need to get rid of this hair."

"Your wish is my command. But don't cut it all off. Men like long hair you know. Especially me."

Hand in hand, they walked to the UPS truck and drove off into the hot afternoon sun."

***

Once Super Cuts cut Rapunzel's hair into a more modern, less heavy style, she agreed to donate her locks to an organization that made wigs for cancer patients.

Rapunzel's parents didn't recognize their daughter at first, but after she was able to answer several questions about her childhood, they embraced her as the long-lost little girl they thought was forever gone.

She introduced them to Bob Prince-Charming and informed them they were getting married soon, surprising everyone including Bob. He blushed but agreed it was a good idea.

The police picked up Gus later that evening, charging him with kidnapping and wrongful confinement of both Rapunzel and Cook. He went to prison for the rest of his life.

Free again, Cook decided to use her skills to start her own cooking show. She became a celebrity on the Food Channel and never looked back. Her cookbook, Candlelight Meals in the Castle, became a bestseller on the New York Times Best Sellers List. She never married, refusing to be tied down ever again, but remained the constant companion to one of the firemen that saved her.

Within weeks Rapunzel and Bob Prince-Charming were married in true fairy tale fashion in a large cathedral surrounded by hundreds of their dearest friends and two or three fairies. They planned to buy the house next door to Rapunzel's parents so she'd never have to be away from them again. Leaving the wedding, they went directly to a luxury ship, beginning their honeymoon.

Their love was beyond any other before or since. Then one afternoon, as they explored a small island at one of their ports of call, Mid-Eastern terrorists bombed their cruise ship, sinking it instantly. The island which was mostly uninhabited had no facilities to call for help so the tourists became stranded.

Rapunzel and Bob built a small hut on a hill that overlooked the water. There they stayed, living on fresh fish and coconuts. Frolicking in the surf and getting brown. Their neighbors lived in other huts farther down the beach. They enjoyed getting together for barbecues and dancing around the fire. All the beaches on the island were considered nude beaches since the saltwater and harsh sun were hard on their clothes.

They sometimes wondered about the loved ones they left behind. But mostly, they enjoyed being together in paradise, where they lived happily ever after.

That's No Bull
By Kathy Akins

HENRY WAINSWORTH LAY FACE DOWN in the dirt. Dead.

His prize Angus bull, Orion, circled the pen charging at anyone who approached the fence. His hooves trampled the dirt surrounding Henry but never touched him.

Sheriff Frank Trammell stood with his hands shoved into his jeans pockets, watching. The brim of his Stetson dipped low to shade his eyes from the morning sun.

"Ain't it the dangest thing you ever seen?" Carl Jameson shook his head as he approached.

Frank accepted a foam cup filled with black coffee from his deputy and sipped the steaming liquid.

"Never thought that ol' bull would turn on Henry," Carl said.

"I don't think he did," Frank said. "Look around, Carl. What's missing?"

Carl scanned the surrounding landscape. "Where's his truck?"

"Exactly."

"Sheriff, if you don't need me any longer, I would like to go finish feeding Henry's cows. He keeps a tight schedule. I mean, kept." Nate Chandler was clearly shaken by that morning's discovery.

"Go ahead, Nate. We can call you if we have any more questions. I'm sorry you had to be the one to find Henry." Frank rested his hand on Nate's shoulder. "I know he was your friend as well as boss."

Nate nodded and then headed toward the battered farm truck loaded with sacks of feed and a few bales of hay.

As soon as the truck cleared the area, the local banker, Joe Cash, with two other men drove up to the pen with a horse trailer. It took them a few minutes, but they coaxed the agitated animal into it. Frank and Carl were inside the pen as soon as the trailer gate latched but found nothing suspicious.

"Guess we'll see what the M.E. has to say about the cause of death," Frank said. "In the meantime, you and I are going to figure out what went on last night. We'll start with the girlfriends. You go see Emma Spears, and I'll talk to Widow Adams."

"Right," Carl said, draping the corral with yellow, crime-scene tape.

Joe strode over to them.

"Couldn't help overhearing your conversation, Sheriff," the banker said. "If you're going to start asking questions, you might want to start with Mrs. Wainsworth."

"He wasn't married," Frank said.

"Well, last week he deposited a large amount of money into a joint savings account that he opened with Jenna Dupree, aka Mrs. Henry Wainsworth." Joe smiled knowingly. "Pretty cozy situation."

"Really?" Frank said. "Carl, change of plans. You talk to both girlfriends and I'll check out Jenna."

Draining his coffee cup in two gulps, Frank turned and headed for his cruiser.

***

Jenna stepped onto her front porch when she heard the vehicle roll to a stop on the gravel drive. She dabbed at her eyes with the fresh tissue she had grabbed on her way outside. Frank stepped out of the car and hesitated a moment. He had known Jenna since grade school. She attracted attention even then. Still pretty as a picture, but now she looked a little road weary.

"Sheriff."

"Jenna." Frank tipped his hat. "I have some bad news, and I need to ask you a few questions."

"I already heard. Come on in." Jenna turned and went back inside the house without waiting for Frank to follow.

Removing his hat as he entered, Frank took a seat on the first chair he came to. While his eyes adjusted to the dim lamplight, he surveyed his surroundings.

Jenna occupied a rocking chair directly across from him. Beside her was a small table littered with prescription bottles and wadded tissues. She wiped her eyes and waited for Frank to speak.

Leaning forward, clutching his hat, Frank said, "I'll get right to the point, Jenna. Henry Wainsworth was found deceased in his bull's pen this morning. The bull was in the pen with him."

Frank kept his eyes on Jenna's face, trying to gage her reaction. Stone cold.

"Jenna?"

Jenna twisted the tissue in her hands.

"I understand that you and Henry opened a joint savings account at the bank last week. Mr. and Mrs. Henry Wainsworth," Frank continued. "Care to explain?"

"We planned to get married this coming weekend." Jenna grabbed a fresh tissue.

"On my way here, my deputy also notified me that there is a pending sale of Orion. Doesn't sound like Henry. He loved that animal." Frank stood and placed his hat on his chair. "Care to enlighten me?" he asked quietly. He wasn't looking at Jenna, but at the small table beside her. He stepped over to it and picked up a pill bottle with Henry's name on it—nitroglycerin tablets. He raised an eyebrow and gazed at Jenna.

Jumping to her feet, Jenna waved her hand before bringing the tissue to her eyes. "With Henry's heart condition, the bull was becoming too much for him to take care of. He needed to sell it."

Frank tightened his grip on the pill bottle.

Jenna began to pace. "It was worth a lot of money as a prize winning bull. We could use that money. Put it to much better use as we start our future together."

Watching the woman before him become more agitated as she talked, Frank slipped the pill bottle into his shirt pocket. "I need the truth, Jenna."

Stopping mid-stride, Jenna stared at Frank. A cruel expression transformed her pretty face. "He loved that bull so much; he couldn't stand to part with it. He even added my name to its registration papers. An act of love, he said, for a wedding gift." She spat out the words. "That foul beast for a wedding gift! What a joke." She blew her nose.

"Were you with him last night, Jenna? At Orion's pen?" Frank asked softly.

She stared at him.

"Because I knew Henry," Frank said. "He never forgot his pills. Why are his pills here and not with him?" She didn't say anything. "Were you down there, Jenna? You know, my team is going to look at everything. If you left any signs, they'll find them."

Jenna took a deep breath and then shrugged. "What does it matter now?"

"What happened?"

She met his eyes defiantly. "We had another argument. We had been fighting for weeks. I had enough of that nasty creature coming before me, and I told him so. Henry kept saying over and over how wonderful it was, how gentle. I have seen it run at too many hired men to believe that. We fought, and I finally told him to take me home. Of course, he had to detour and say goodnight to the filthy animal. He kept saying he would show me how gentle that creature was. When he went into the pen, I about lost it. He stumbled locking the gate, and his nitro pills fell out of his pocket. When he crumpled to the ground, I reached down and picked them up. He was clutching his chest and saying, 'Orion, Orion' over and over. Not my name. Orion's. I had the pill bottle in my hand, but Orion was who he was calling for. I was done. Orion could have him. I walked away."

Frank no longer recognized the woman before him. "And Henry's truck?"

"Behind the house." A look of defeat softened her harsh expression.

"I think we need to finish this conversation at the station, Jenna." Frank pulled out his handcuffs and began reciting the Miranda warning. Sometimes he hated his job.

The End of a Story
By Stephen B. Bagley

THIS IS HOW A STORY ENDED.

Eve walked into Milligan's with her friend Bette, and as always, her eyes searched the restaurant for his shoulders and that ratty leather jacket and his soft worn hat that felt like velvet when she touched it. For seven weeks, she had searched all their places. The coffee shop, the bookstore, the library, the pier, the Seafood Shack. But Jeremy had disappeared from her life.

She had picked up the phone to call him at work a hundred times, but she lacked the courage. It would be easier on her pride if she ran into him somewhere. Pride often seemed to be all she had now.

She didn't know how to live without him, but she was trying to learn. She took a gym class, went out to movies with Bette and her other friends, and focused on work, turning out reports with an efficiency that even her usually oblivious boss noticed. A couple of guys—Kevin from Sales and Joel from Receivable—asked her out, and she said yes. Nice enough dates, and she had enjoyed them. Kevin even made her laugh, and Joel was sweet. But she kissed them good night at the door.

Bette threaded her way through the crowd, looking for a table. Eve followed, wondering when she would stop feeling that pit in her stomach when she didn't see him. She stumbled and caught herself on the edge of a table. The men seated at it smiled at her. She apologized, backed away, turned toward Bette, and saw Jeremy.

He didn't see her. He stood by a table talking to two other men. The crowd closed between them, and she lost sight of him. For a moment, she paused, her heart pounding. Then she pushed forward, leaving Bette behind, weaving her way forcefully toward her last chance.

"Jeremy," she said.

He turned and saw her. He started to smile, but it faded away.

"Eve," he said. "How are you?"

"Fine," she said. But that wasn't what she meant to say. She meant to say she was falling to pieces, her heart broke, her life in shambles, but the words wouldn't come.

"Where's Ben?" he asked.

"I don't know," she said. "Back with his wife, I guess. We're not together."

Jeremy paused and then nodded. "Sorry to hear that."

"I broke up with him," Eve said, wanting him to understand. "I sent him away. I remembered what you said. 'If he cheats on his wife, why wouldn't he cheat on you?' I should have listened."

"He cheated on you," Jeremy asked with anger in his voice.

Surely that meant something, she thought. "No, but I realized he would. I realized the love of his life was him." She laughed.

Jeremy took a deep breath. "I'm sorry to hear things didn't work out. It's good to see you." He shifted his shoulders awkwardly. "Well, I've got to go. I'm leaving New York in a couple of days. I have a lot of packing still to do. Got a new job in Seattle."

"Oh," she said. "Seattle. Good. Good. Is it one you wanted?"

"It's a good job," he said. "It rains a lot out there, but I'll get used to it, they say." He grinned.

She laughed to keep from crying. *He's moved on*, she thought. *He's moving away*.

"It's good to see you," he said. "You look...beautiful." He smiled. "Take care of yourself. Tell your parents I said hi."

"I will," she said. "You take care, too. Enjoy that rain."

And he walked away while she stood in a crowd of strangers and she realized that would be her life—to always be alone in a crowd.

"No!" she said. She took three quick steps and grabbed his arm. "Jeremy, wait."

He turned back, his face surprised. "What?"

She couldn't find the words.

"What, Eve?" He sighed at her silence. "I really need to go."

"Okay," she said. "I understand. But can we talk outside? Just for a minute."

He looked down at the floor. "I don't think that would be a good idea. Don't you think we've hurt each other more than enough?"

She swallowed. "Just for a minute. I need to tell you a few things. It won't take long."

He took a deep breath. "For a minute."

They found a bench in the tiny park across the street.

"Okay," Jeremy said. "What do you want from me, Eve?"

"Nothing," she said, but her heart called her a liar. "I needed to apologize."

"No," he said. "No. I don't want to do this."

"Please," she said. "I need to say how sorry I am. How I would give anything to go back and fix things."

"Eve, we're—"

"I know you're not in love with me anymore," she said. "I know we can't go back. That you don't want to. You've moved on. Good. I'm glad. I want you to be happy." She could feel the tears behind her eyes threatening to overflow. "I wanted you to know I will always want the best for you."

He looked away.

She wiped her eyes. Time to go. Time to walk away. Time to let him walk away. Time to face the bleakness ahead. She needed a few moments to gather her strength.

He stood and took a couple of steps away. She wanted to weep, but she didn't. This was the result of her decisions. She had made them, and she would live with them. She had enough courage to do that.

She rose. "I'd better let you go. I'm sorry if I hurt you."

He turned, his face shadowed. "I'm at a place in my life—"

"You don't have to explain," she said. "I understand." She shook her head and wiped her eyes. "We had something lovely, and I broke it. I didn't mean to. But that doesn't mean anything. I wanted you to know I miss you. Oh how I do."

"Let me finish," he said. "I'm at a place in my life where there are more goodbyes than hellos. More people lost than found."

She watched him, almost afraid to breathe.

"Comes with getting older," he said with a short laugh. "You can't imagine how...lost I've felt without you. How empty. Then I saw you with him, and I was angry. It was better to be angry than empty. But now...."

He was silent for longer than she could bear, but she bore it anyway. *Please, God, please*, she prayed. *Another chance, and I won't blow it. Please, oh please.*

"Too many goodbyes," he said finally. "Not enough hellos. I don't want that for my life. I don't want to tell you goodbye." He looked at her. "Hello. How are you? I missed you. I *missed* you."

She sobbed and launched herself into his eager arms.

This is how a story ended, and a new one began.

The Helper
By Wendy Blanton

ELIZABETH WALKED INTO HER OFFICE with her coffee and stopped in the doorway. The Chinese vase she'd moved from the foyer to the credenza behind her desk was gone. Again.

Sighing, she put the cup on the desk and walked back through the gallery. It was on the round table in the center of the foyer. Again. Clenching her jaw, she took it back to her office, placed it deliberately on the credenza, and turned on her computer.

Rather than starting with the calendar, she opened her digital to do list and added "Tell cleaning staff to stop moving the stupid vase" to the queue, which was getting longer by the day.

Outside the birds chirped in the early spring sun. It wasn't quite warm enough to open windows, but it would be soon. The view through the leaded windows showed the trees starting to bud. When she'd inherited her family mansion, she'd spent hours drinking in the view, watching the leaves change and fall, and then snow falling in fat flakes.

Her work load had changed from managing contractors to managing her schedule. Wedding season was around the corner, and her marketing had worked, perhaps a little too well.

She had weddings in various places on the grounds every weekend from late May to early August. The bridal showers were in full swing, no doubt with baby showers to follow.

The phone rang and startled her out of her chair. Taking a deep breath to calm herself, she picked it up. "Thank you for calling Ridgecrest Manor. This is Elizabeth."

"Betsy! This is Aunt Gertie."

Elizabeth's heart skipped a beat, and she faked a smile. "Aunt Gertie! It's so good to hear from you!"

"How are you, dear? And how are things going there?"

"Busy, and getting busier by the day."

"Well, I won't keep you, then. I wonder if we might hold Amanda's bridal shower there?"

"The shower too?"

"We thought it might simplify things to have the same venue for the shower and the reception, and after all, it is the family mansion."

It's mine now. Uncle Henry knew you all would sell it.

"That depends on when you want to schedule it."

"How about the last Saturday in March?"

Elizabeth looked at the calendar. "In two weeks? Will that give you enough time to get everything together?"

"Oh, sure. We have most everything done now. We'd just have to contact everyone about the change of location. The church double-booked the hall, so we're in a bit of a pinch. Are you open that day?"

"I am." *Sadly.* "What time do you want to start?"

"Two o'clock, if that suits you. I assume we'll get the friends and family discount?"

"Of course."

"Good. We'll bring the food, so it will be extra easy for you."

She pinched the bridge of her nose. "Who's catering?" *Not Busby's. Not Busby's.*

"Busby's, of course. We use them for everything."

"I know you love them! I'll email the paperwork to you."

"Lovely, dear. See you soon."

She hung up the phone and groaned. Picking up her personal cell phone, she scrolled through her messages to the group text with her best friends from college.

All hands on deck! My aunt just scheduled Amanda's shower here in 2 weeks! Can you all come for dinner? I'll make pizza.

The answers flooded back within minutes.

Emma**: I'm in!**

Ashley: **Me too.**

Courtney: **I have to shuffle some stuff. I might be fashionably late.**

Ashley: **You always are.**

***

Precisely at 6:00, three cars followed the hairpin turns of Seven Curves Ridge Road. She could see them from the picture window in her kitchen as she tossed the salad and put the pizza in the oven.

Her great aunt and uncle had remodeled the kitchen a few years before to bring it up to date and up to code. It reminded her of the small kitchens she'd seen in Europe—homey and rustic—but on a larger scale, with a breakfast nook in the picture window at the back of the kitchen, overlooking the formal garden and the valley beyond.

She had the table set, and the kitchen smelled like cheese and basil when the cars parked outside the kitchen door. They let themselves in, chattering as they hung coats and kicked off boots next to the door.

Ashley came to the quartz-topped island and handed Elizabeth a bottle. "I thought we might need this."

Elizabeth laughed. "Great minds." She opened the fridge and took out an identical bottle, putting Ashley's in the door to chill. She passed Ashley the corkscrew.

"Will you do the honors?"

"Certainly."

Emma and Courtney joined them as Elizabeth got stemless wine glasses from the cupboard.

As Ashley poured wine, Courtney leaned on the counter and grinned. "So, Amanda's shower! This should be exciting!"

Emma rolled her eyes. "Aunt Gertie wants the family discount, right?"

"Of course. I'm lucky she's not needling me to do it free since it's," she made air quotes, "the family house."

Courtney snorted. "If they're not paying to help with the upkeep, it's not the family house."

"I know that, and you know that, but it's going to take a decade or so to get it across to the rest of the family."

They took their wine to the table, and Elizabeth noted to herself that she needed to get in touch with the gardening staff ASAP.

"You know what I think you should do?" asked Ashley.

"What?"

"Take all of the pricing off your website and put in a form for a quote. Then make the friends and family rate ten percent higher than the normal rate."

Courtney giggled. "Did you mean higher?"

"I did."

Elizabeth grinned and got up as the timer beeped. "I like that idea. Thanks for coming on short notice. I need you all to help me with the catering policy."

Emma groaned. "Oh, no. She's using Busby's."

"She is."

"No! Your kitchen is going to smell like fried chicken for days!" said Ashley.

"Maybe," said Courtney. "It depends on the menu they can manage on site. You don't have fryers here."

"I don't, and I won't," said Elizabeth. "That's what I need you to help me with." She cut the pizza and brought it to the table.

"Where's your laptop?" asked Courtney.

"In the office." She took a legal pad from the stand on the counter beside the fridge. "I have this for notes."

"Good girl. Let's divide and conquer."

***

A week later, they met again to discuss progress. This time, they gathered in Elizabeth's sitting room with wine, cheese, and pastries.

"Wow, fancy," said Courtney.

"I'm testing the food for another shower," said Elizabeth, sinking into her favorite chair with her feet curled under her.

Courtney snorted. "You mean you have a client who will trust you with the food?"

"Several, actually, and none of them are related to me."

"Figures," said Emma. "Hey, are your cleaning people using a new furniture polish? It smelled extra lemony when I came through the gallery."

Elizabeth frowned. "No, in fact they didn't come this week. Something about staffing, but they'll send extra people next week."

"Really?" asked Ashley. "I was thinking the whole place looked especially clean. I guess you decided to keep that vase on the foyer table? I thought you had it in your office."

Elizabeth sighed and took a drink of wine. "I don't know who keeps moving it back."

"Is the house haunted?" asked Courtney.

"Not that I know of. We better get down to business before I drink too much. Anyone want to go first?"

"I will," said Ashley. "The website is done, and your social media posts are scheduled for the rest of the month. Now if someone wants to know how much things cost, there's an email form with specific questions so you—or I, or someone—can give a quote."

"Good. Now as long as none of my relatives have a screen shot of the old site, I'm covered."

"Well, to be honest, the prices on the old site weren't very accurate since we did them early on. We actually over-estimated in most cases, so if they do have screen shots, their cost will actually be a little bit less."

"Bonus!" said Courtney, raising her glass in a toast.

Ashley grinned. "I know, so you really can charge them more if you want to. I've updated the price lists, too, and cleaned up the policy book."

"That's it? That's all you did?" asked Emma, grinning cheekily.

Ashley shrugged. "I had a slow day at the office. How about you, Em?"

"I'll let Elizabeth tell you about our meeting with Busby's." She grinned as Elizabeth snorted. "I re-organized the butler's pantry so it's now the off-site caterer room. They have plenty of work space and a couple of electric burners. I cleaned the warming ovens and moved everything you don't want them to touch to the silver safe or the kitchen."

"Thank goodness," said Elizabeth. "Most of it was put away anyway, but now they won't be able to help themselves to what's in the cabinets. Did we get the compostable plates and utensils?"

Emma laughed. "I did, and they're in the cupboards. Also, I've cleared my schedule for the day of the shower so I can be here to help."

"To laugh at my family, you mean."

"They are entertaining," said Courtney.

"For you, maybe! What about you?"

"Your security system has been upgraded. There are cameras in the non-customer areas and new locks and alarms on the doors."

"Alarms?" asked Emma.

Courtney laughed. "Oh, yeah. Not only are they loud enough to hear downstairs when they go off, they'll trigger cameras to start recording so you'll have video of Aunt Gertie trying to get into the upstairs rooms."

Emma laughed and high-fived her.

"I haven't turned the alarms on yet. Do you want to hear them?"

"Yes!" said Emma and Ashley together.

Courtney set her glass on the coffee table and left the room. A moment later, they heard a beep and "Level Nine Authorization Required."

They burst into laughter as it repeated. When it shut off and Courtney came back, Emma said, "Girl, where did you get that?"

Courtney scowled at her. "Star Trek: The Next Generation, of course. Luddite. By the way, I have an app for your phone that will shut off the alarm and recording separately. It will keep going until you shut it off." She settled back in her chair. "So, Bets, your turn. Start with Busby's."

Emma smiled and tucked her feet under her, cradling her wine glass in both hands. "Y'all are going to love this."

Elizabeth topped off her glass. "Well, to start with, Mr. Busby himself came with his catering manager, and they were late."

"Late?" gasped Ashley.

"I know. We brought them through the front door to the butler's pantry and explained the new policy—we didn't tell them it's new, of course—about access to the full kitchen being available only to Ridgeview Manor staff. They asked if there would be a staff member available on the day. I started to stammer because they took me by surprise, but Emma whisked in and said she's the kitchen manager, and sadly, she has to go out of town that weekend to spell her sister, who takes care of their mother with dementia."

Courtney laughed. "Emma! You don't have a sister, and your mother is sharper than we are!"

"She also lives in Arkansas and will likely never meet Mr. Busby."

Elizabeth grinned. "It was inspired. Really. Even I believed her. Anyway, they were peeved about not having kitchen access. The manager, Mr. Dumfrie—"

Courtney's jaw sagged. "Dumfries?!"

"Yeah, do you know him?"

"No, but Dum—fries!"

"I know. He's a boot licker. So he takes some papers out of his jacket pocket and starts flipping through them, and he's like, 'But, but Mrs. Conner has fried chicken and hush puppies on the menu! She's expecting a hundred guests! We can't possibly do all that ahead of time!' In my best customer service voice, I said was so sorry, but fried chicken wouldn't have happened anyway since we don't have fryers, but maybe they'd agree to ham and potato salad. He sputtered something about Mrs. Conner being very particular. I reminded him that she's my aunt, and that I was sure she would accept a refund of her deposit if they couldn't work something out.

"At that point, Mr. Busby was ticked and threatened to not cater here at all. I said that was his right, and he got downright ugly, which I expected. So I let him bluster about his years in the business and lack of experience on my part, how I could learn a thing or two from him, while I gathered up my southern charm. It was a pure pleasure to interrupt him to say it might be better if he doesn't cater here. I worked events his business catered when I was in college and spent many hours cleaning up after his staff. The extra pay was helpful, but the customer was always the one who got the big cleaning bill. He was turning red in the face by then, so I said I'd send the cleaning bill to him instead of the customer if they left my venue in such a state."

They all laughed, and Courtney leaned over for a high five. "You go, girl! What did he say?"

"He sputtered and walked out. Mr. Dumfries puffed up like an angry peacock and said they do as much as they can in the time allotted, and I said they need to contract more time to clean up after themselves so they can leave the venue in the condition they found it in and cut him off when he tried to say he did. Then he sputtered and left." She laughed. "You should have heard the call I got from Aunt Gertie that afternoon! Wooo, she blistered my ears, and I calmly told her I was sorry my policy ruined her menu, and if she wanted to have me handle the food instead of Busby's, I'd need to know by today, but that I have no way to fry chicken for a hundred people."

"What did she say? Did she call to have you do the food?" asked Courtney.

"She did not. She changed caterers since Mr. Busby has officially blacklisted us. They're doing ham and potato salad, by the way. She did say Amanda will be sorely disappointed, and they might have to rethink the wedding venue. Darn it. That would open up a day I can host the wedding of someone who's not a bridezilla from hell. Or maybe give me a Saturday off."

***

After they left, Elizabeth thought about Courtney's off-hand question about the house being haunted. She went downstairs and moved as many of the heirloom dust-collectors as she could find. She locked the vase from the foyer table in the adjacent curio cabinet and replaced it with another one. Then she went to bed.

The next morning, she took her coffee cup and walked through the house. Everything had been put back.

She frowned. "Huh. Maybe Courtney was onto something." She looked around. "Good morning, ghost! If you're the one doing the dusting and polishing, you're doing a great job. If there's a way to let me know what you're doing, that would be great so I don't pay the cleaners to do it. Oh, and I know you love that vase on the foyer table, but I keep moving it because I love it, too, and I don't want it to get broken. Could we compromise and use that spot for the things we agree can be broken?"

A truck pulled into the circular drive and parked. The logo on the side said Spiced Pear Catering. "Of course the caterer is early. Good thing I'm dressed, eh, ghost?" She went to the door and opened it as a young woman got out.

"Good morning! I'm so sorry to be early! I didn't know how long it would take me to get here. My map app isn't reliable for estimating time."

Elizabeth stepped outside as the woman came up the steps. "It's fine. I'm Elizabeth Conner."

The woman stuck out her hand. "Nice to meet you. I'm Hannah Curry."

Elizabeth shook her hand. "Come on in. I'll show you around."

"Do you mind if I take pictures? I won't actually be here for the shower. My boss will be here."

"Sure, whatever you need to do."

***

The morning of the shower, Aunt Gertie arrived an hour ahead of when she was supposed to. Elizabeth saw her car coming up the road and went to greet her when she parked in front of the door.

Unloading several boxes and bags into the foyer, she said, "Now, Betsy, you just do what you need to do. I'm going to do a little decorating." She picked up a pair of totes. "Ball room?"

"It's all ready for you."

"I never doubted." She walked past the foyer table and stopped, pointing to the gaudy vase with blown glass roses sitting there. "Where's Mother Conner's vase?"

Elizabeth nodded at the curio cabinet. "I locked it up so it doesn't get broken."

"Why did you choose this one to replace it?"

"I thought it looked nice."

Aunt Gertie smiled. "It does, doesn't it? I gave that to her for their 50th."

"Then I chose well."

Aunt Gertie hummed in agreement and headed into the gallery as Courtney walked over.

She looked at the anniversary vase and whispered, "What is that?"

"You were right. There's a ghost. I asked if we could use that spot for things we want to get knocked off and broken, and the next morning, that was there."

Courtney snickered. "Whose ghost is it?"

"I don't know yet, but I don't think they like Aunt Gertie."

"I like them already. I'm getting coffee. Do you want some?"

"Yeah, thanks, I'll be in my office."

A few minutes later, Courtney set a mug on her desk. "You might want to check on your aunt at some point. I hear muttering coming from that direction. I'm going upstairs to make sure everything is working right."

"Thanks." She picked up the mug and sipped as she scrolled through her emails. She heard music start—some awful opera. The volume turned down, and several minutes later, it went up. Again, it turned down gradually before turning up. It continued for the next hour, and her aunt's muttering got louder.

Finally, the music turned off and her aunt stormed down the hall. "Betsy! What on earth is the matter with your wifi?"

She frowned and looked up as Aunt Gertie stepped into the doorway looking like a flustered hen. "My wifi? Nothing, as far as I know."

"Something keeps turning my Bluetooth speaker down."

"Bluetooth doesn't use wifi. It's a different signal."

Aunt Gertie snorted. "A signal is a signal, dear. Do please check your router. Oh, and do you have any tape? Mine has gone missing."

"Sure." She picked up the tape dispenser and took it to her.

"Thank you, dear. Now maybe I can get something done." She turned and bustled back to the ball room.

Frowning, Elizabeth picked up her cell phone and sent a message to Courtney: **Does Bluetooth use wifi?**

Courtney: **No. Why?**

Tell you later.

Courtney: **There's a catering truck coming up the drive.**

Elizabeth took a long sip of her coffee and went to let them in.

When she opened the door, she saw a tall man with dark hair directing several people about what to take in first. She smiled. Tall, dark, and hopefully handsome.

He turned, and her smile turned fake. Walking down the steps, she said, "Well, Joshua Bartlett. I didn't know you were the pear in Spiced Pear Catering."

The side of his mouth quirked up. "You must be a College of the Ozarks alum."

She scowled. "Are you implying that I didn't graduate?"

He reached in his back pocket and took out his wallet. "I would never do such a thing. I'm implying you've mistaken me for my twin brother." He held up his driver's license.

Her mouth went dry. "Jefferson Bartlett."

He leaned toward her and said, "Call me Jeff. Josh is the evil twin."

Her face felt hot. "Now that you mention it, I do remember him making a big deal about having a twin. Almost as big a deal as being called Joshua. He never answered when any of us called him Josh."

"I'm the only one he'll tolerate it from. Even our mother can't call him Josh."

"Wow. Come in, and I'll show you to the work space."

His employees had gathered near the door, laden with boxes and baskets. He followed her in as if she were the only person around. "Hannah showed me the pictures. I've been looking forward to working in that space all week."

"Have you? That's nice to hear. So, wait, Hannah Curry? Is she the spice in the name?"

"Not yet. Her dad is my partner."

She grinned. "Bartlett and Curry. Spiced pear. Very clever."

"If you think that's clever, you should try the curried pears we developed for our signature dessert."

"Sounds delicious." Her face warmed again as he chuckled.

As she neared the door to the butler's pantry, her aunt's voice echoed through the gallery.

"Oh, for goodness' sake!"

Jeff chuckled. "That doesn't sound good."

Elizabeth sighed. "No. The space is just through here." She took two more steps and pushed the door open.

"Thanks. We'll manage if you need to go see what that's about."

She rolled her eyes. "It's my aunt being dramatic. Have you met her yet?"

"I did have that pleasure!" He chuckled. "Go on. No doubt she needs you more than I do."

"I'll check on you in a bit. Just to make sure you have everything you need." She backed away. "In the space. For food prep."

He winked at her. She couldn't stop the grin as she turned and strode through the gallery to find her aunt rifling through her totes. "Something wrong?"

Aunt Gertie jumped and whirled, her hands pressed to her ample bosom. "Betsy! You scared me!"

"Sorry, it just sounds like you're having trouble with something."

"I can't find my keys! I never take them out of my purse except to use them, and now they're gone!"

Elizabeth frowned and looked around. A set of keys rested in the empty punchbowl. She picked them up. "You mean these keys?"

Aunt Gertie looked over her shoulder. "Where did you find them?"

"Here, on the table."

"Oh my word. I must be more scatter-brained than I thought today." She laughed. "Being back here after all this time must have me spooked. If I didn't know better, I'd say your grandmother was pranking me."

"Why would Nana prank you? I didn't think you spent that much time with her."

"Oh, no, Grandmother Conner. My mother-in-law never really liked me, but you wouldn't know that since she died before you were born." She walked toward the door. "I need to get a few more things, and I'll move my car."

"Thanks. Um, Aunt Gertie, did Grandma Conner die here?"

"In the ballroom? Oh, no, she was upstairs in her bed." She turned and walked into the gallery.

Elizabeth waited for her footsteps to fade. "Grandma Conner, is that you?"

The Bluetooth speaker came on, and jazz music played at a low volume:

'And latch on to the affirmative, don't mess with mister in-between.' The speaker shut off.

Elizabeth laughed. "Maybe this day won't be a train wreck after all."

The Tree King and the Stone Girl
By D.E. Chandler

ONCE IN THE VERY FIRST BREATHS of air on Earth, a stone girl was pushed up from beneath her earthen covers as Gaia shook herself to regain comfort in her great slumber. Stone Girl found herself covered in only water at first, but soon many new things came and went in the water all around her. There were slimy things, and scaly things, armored things, and shelled things.

For a time, she was kept company by a colony of creatures that seemed to be partly made of stone, and she wondered at their compatibility, and the way they nestled together, much like the crystals that made up her own form. They required nourishment besides the light of Solus above and the breath of Gaia filtering through the sea. They ate the tiny things that swam past. The excess from this they used to attach themselves to the stone girl and build more dwellings for more creatures.

Then, slowly, the water retreated, and the rains slowly washed away the remains of the sea creatures, and the stone girl was left alone. Solus, Luna, and the rain-bringers were the only sights to keep her company, and Gaia's song was all she heard. Gaia, Luna, and Solus danced many dances, and it seemed that their triple courtship would go on for eternity, and that stone girl would have to watch, forever lonely, though never alone.

Then, one night, when Luna was coming up to peek around Gaia's shoulder, the west wind carried some small hint of something new. The scent that drifted to her was alive, like the ocean, but dry like the land. It was fresh and new and—green.

Slowly, new creatures came to see Stone Girl, and though none of them stayed, they all left her something to remember them by. The shiny winged creatures left her their leftovers from dinner. The scaly creatures came and made their nest just under her east face, and once their young hatched, they left her the eggshells. By and by though, each animal that came would leave her. She felt the changes around her, the deposits left by all of her friends over the seasons piled up somewhat, but then other creatures began coming to take bits of it away. These creatures were small. Some had jointed bodies and armor like the ocean creatures, though they seemed to be made differently.

Some were long and thin with soft bodies and no eyes. They would use the bits for sustenance, the way the ocean creatures had consumed each other. They, in turn, would leave their own smaller deposits.

Some days, clouds would cover Sol's face, and Stone Girl could not see him or Luna. She worried for Gaia, though she did not feel that Gaia was afraid. The rains would come, and the scent of the green would come with them, closer and closer every season. On the season that the green arrived, just after a spring rain, Stone Girl became aware of a strange movement in the deposits all around her. They had become as familiar to her as the blanket of Gaia had been before her surfacing. They had grown so deep they nearly reached her middle. And now, new creatures, green creatures with probing tentacles that clung to the deposits grew, and died, leaving their bodies to loosen the deposits all around her.

One season the rains came so heavy that some of the soil washed away. Later, Gaia grumbled and shifted in her sleep. Stone Girl rode high into the sky, so far up, she was afraid she might pierce the rain bringers. The rain bringers roared at her, flashing and sending their fire lashes through the air at her. Stone girl grew very afraid. The rain battered her face, wearing it down.

The next season larger green ones came, and this time at Solus' retreat, only some died. Some merely slept, their deep roots still pulsing with life. This was a comfort to Stone Girl. In particular one of the green ones that was closest to her.

Each season his roots grew deeper, and he grew taller, his spreading branches shading her from Solus' close times and drawing the fire lashes of the rain bringers away from her. He seemed to hum to her, and one season, he spoke.

"I am here. I am for you. We are together now." His roots thrummed the message, and she felt it in the vibrations of her crystals.

"Together! Yes," she felt herself pulse back. "Together." Soon, she relaxed into the embrace of his roots, and was, for many seasons content in his company. Then one season, it seemed that he had grown so great, he overshadowed all of the other green ones.

"You are so much more than the others," Stone Girl said. "They die, and you do not."

"I am a king among my kind," he replied. "A king must live a long time and bear many burdens."

"A long time, but not like Sol, Luna, and Gaia."

"No," he said. "I will die one day. Long before you cease to be."

Stone Girl was saddened by the thought of losing her beloved Tree King.

She hardly noticed the spring rains when they came that season. Though Tree King's leaves were as green as any other year, it seemed there were fewer than last time. The thought of losing him was with her always. She grew quiet.

Tree King sensed this and many other things, but he waited, patient and strong, for her to come to acceptance. Through that season the rains lashed at the mountain peak they shared, soil rolled away layer after layer. Tree King tightened his roots around Stone Girl and sent them deep into the mountain, finding other, larger, quieter stones to use as leverage.

All the time she spent contemplating the loss of her Tree King, it never occurred to her that anything might tear them apart other than his eventual death. By the time she realized she was in danger, she hung far over the edge of the cliff only about a third of her weight rested on the mountain.

"You are here."

"Yes."

"You are for me?"

"Yes."

"You won't let me fall?"

"Never."

And to this day, many thousands of years later, the roots of Tree King still hold Stone Girl aloft over the great valley. Though he is many, many seasons dead, his promise to her is still alive.

Excerpt from the novel
Dawn Before The Dark
By Wendy Blanton

TANWEN RODE HER DRAGON, Quillon, to the Keep. She was glad to be going over the woods instead of through them. The air carried the scents of mid-summer flowers and smoke from cook fires. She could see men coming in from the fields, their hands shielding their eyes to block their view of Quillon.

Look left, beloved, Quillon said telepathically.

She shaded her eyes as she turned toward the setting sun, and saw a pair of dragons with riders coming toward them. One had red hair that matched her own.

Who is she riding?

That is Saphir. The other dragon is Peio, but I am unsure who the rider is.

She smiled. *I think it's Magda.*

That is logical. Peio enjoys her company, as Saphir enjoys Aithne's.

Do you think Saphir will Choose Aithne?

That is not for me to say, but I have encouraged it.

Saphir and Peio fell into formation with Quillon, and he led them home.

The stone walls of the Keep glowed pink in the late afternoon light as Quillon circled over the landing pad. Peio and Saphir circled higher, waiting for their turns.

When Quillon landed, Tanwen unstrapped herself from the saddle and trotted down the steps, the scent of sunbaked stone greeting her. She ducked under the ledge of the landing pad, and Quillon launched to make room for Saphir. The wind from his wings stirred the dust on the roof, and she sneezed as she headed for the stairs into the Keep.

She waited on the first landing, and a moment later she heard Aithne walking down the steps.

"Did you find anything, Mama?"

"Yes, unfortunately. Another burned homestead a few leagues from here."

"That's five now, isn't it?"

"Yes. What were you doing out?"

"Magda wanted to work on the maneuver she messed up during her leadership mission." She turned back to the stairs as Magda came down.

"Did you get it figured out?" asked Tanwen.

"We did, thanks to Peio and Saphir," said Magda.

"Excellent. I look forward to seeing it. Aithne, I have to report to Arwyne. Dinner in an hour?"

"Shouldn't we wait for Papa?"

"He came to look over the site, so he won't be back for a few more hours. He said we should eat without him."

Aithne shrugged. "Can we make it an hour and a half? We were in the air for a long time, and I'm frozen through."

"Of course." She squeezed Aithne's shoulder. "Go take a hot bath."

The girls clattered down the stairs ahead of her. Tanwen went down two flights and turned right at the hallway.

The first door on the left was different than the others in the Keep. Hewn centuries before from a single Gerdin tree, the wood was gray with age and carved with knots that flowed from one to the next. She ran her hand over the surface before knocking.

"Come in."

She found Arwyne, the liaison between the Keep and Dragon councils, next to the bay windows across from the door. She wore her customary midnight blue robes, and her silver hair was braided. She had a large book in her lap and two more open on the low table beside her.

"Arwyne, we found another one."

Arwyne's brow creased. "Where?"

Tanwen walked to the map on the wall. "There." She picked up a pin and marked the spot as someone knocked at the door. One of the teachers opened it and peered inside. "Wybren Arwyne, is this a good time?"

Arwyne sighed. "Not particularly, but since I'm sure you have them all out there, you might as well bring them in. Tanwen, I'm sorry, but this should only take a few minutes."

"Of course." She leaned against the wall and crossed her arms as two teachers herded a dozen children into the study. The children looked at Arwyne, round-eyed, and she smiled at them. Tanwen grinned at how easily Arwyne covered her crankiness, but truth be told, she wanted to hear the story again, too.

"Come in, children, where you can hear me."

The teachers arranged the children on the floor at her feet before moving to stand, one against each wall, ready to remove anyone who misbehaved. Wybren Arwyne's study was the last place for foolery.

Arwyne leaned forward a little. "Children, hear the story of your past. In the beginning, our world was barren and lifeless. Cruthadair, Mother Creator, cast her eye about the stars. She saw our world and formed it into a life-giving planet, filled with food and comfort and love. In those days, everyone used magic to perform simple chores and healing.

"For generations, people lived in peace. The first ones taught their children about Cruthadair's love. Each generation talked less about Cruthadair and more about her children: Brigid, goddess of hearth and home; Maccha, her bloodthirsty sister, who eats the flesh of her slain enemies and dominates her lovers through cunning and guile; and their brother, Laoch, god of warriors, heroes, and champions.

"After a time, one man became envious of his neighbor. He took what he coveted by force, and his neighbor gathered others and went to take it back. No one knows what the object was, or why it was so dear that it was worth the blood spilled. One killing sparked another until all of Balphrahn was at war.

"The dragons observed all of this, and when it appeared mankind would exterminate itself, they intervened, some on one side and some on the other as they saw fit. More blood was spilled, and thousands died in dragon fire." She raised her eyebrows and paused for effect as the children shivered.

"Eventually, one side overpowered the other. Who can say if it was the right side or the wrong side? The vanquished fled east, through the woods and across the wide river. Eventually, they called their new home Aramach, and their descendants are those who harry our border to this day.

"The strongest of the dragon riders was chosen to sit on the throne and rule over all of Slan. He ordered a grand castle built in the center of the land we know as Slan, and from there, he led everyone to prosperity.

"King Fergus ruled wisely. At first. As time passed, his power overcame him and he cast his eye on his fellow dragon riders. He decreed that, as king, it was his right to have concubines and chose the female dragon riders as his own.

"Some of the women went to him willingly, smitten with his

countenance and charm. Others went willingly because of his power and the knowledge that if they caught his child, they could mother the next monarch.

"One did not go willingly. Ailin protested, saying she was in love with another and wished to stay faithful to him. King Fergus ignored her pleas. His guards brought her to his chamber, where he overpowered her and took her by force.

"When it was done, he laughed at Ailin's tears and dismissed her. Instead of leaving, she stood next to his bed and cursed all men through the power of her magic and rage--and in the name of Maccha--with a dread of dragons and cowardice. As Maccha moved to grant her wish, Laoch intervened, offended at the curse on one of his own. He was able to keep the cowardice from future generations, but not the dread of dragons. In retribution, he took magic from all women. A great cry went up in all of Balphrahn and Brigid took pity, blessing women with her healing touch.

"King Fergus rose, terrified, from his bed and ran from the castle. His dragon, seeing the cowardice upon him, repudiated him, burning his curse away with dragon fire."

The children gasped as a silver dragon flew past the window, heading for the lairs.

"If it had been only King Fergus who was repudiated, it would have been bad enough, but all the male dragon riders suffered the same fate. The bond between dragon and rider is stronger than those of a mother and her child. The dragons who were strongly bonded to their male riders also died. Those who were not bonded as strongly lived, but fled to the mountains in grief.

"A great cry went up. When Ailin realized what she had done, she fled to the woods, too ashamed to face her lover and friends. When they found her, she was great with child and insensible with grief and shame.

"The remaining members of the Dragon Council judged Ailin harshly and banished her far to the west, beyond the mountains. She did not go alone, for her friends were also banished. They were escorted many leagues to the mountains and through a pass, never to be seen again. It is because of the Curse of Ailin that, to this day, only women ride the dragons, and only the men are mages."

The teachers stepped in. "Thank you, Wybren Arwyne. We appreciate your time." They gathered the children and herded them through the exact center of the room where there was nothing to touch.

"It's my pleasure," said Arwyne. She held the smile until they all left.

When the door shut, Tanwen pushed away from the wall and applauded. Arwyne scowled, and Tanwen laughed. "Is that part of the liaison job?"

"Sadly, it is. I'm not sure when it became part of it, but apparently the story has more impact when it comes from an old mouth."

"I've always felt there was more to the story. I've heard it all my life, and it's always the same. No matter who tells it, there is no variation, and it's not like that with any other story I've heard. It's like a slogan of some kind that we dare not change a syllable of in case the gods are listening and punish us for getting it wrong."

Arwyne scoffed. "The gods stopped talking to me long ago."

She levered herself, grunting, from her chair and joined Tanwen at the map. "It seems to be in the same general area so far. What did you find?"

"Three male bodies, the house was branded, and they took cows and horses but left the chickens, same as before."

"No blood?"

"Not on the bodies, and not much elsewhere. Enough to account for wounded, I suppose. Siril and Liam agreed it was the work of a single necromancer."

Arwyne cursed under her breath. "That makes five sites in total, yes?"

"Yes."

"I wonder if the mages all sense the same necromancer? Or if it's a team of them going hither and yon?"

"They've read the same magic signature at all the sites. It's one mage."

"I wonder where he's from. Logic suggests he's from Aramach. Who else would have a reason to attack in Slan? It does seem awfully far west for someone from Aramach. I wonder if they've had these attacks at the Eastern Keep?" She shrugged. "I'll write to Ceann. There isn't much else I can do at this point. Since you're here, take a look at this." She picked up a parchment and handed it to her.

"What is this?" asked Tanwen.

"Something that was brought to my attention recently."

Tanwen skimmed what appeared to be a poem that talked about dragons and warriors. "It seems prophetic, but it must have happened already if the warrior is male."

"Or it's about to happen." Arwyne sighed and went back to her chair. "Nothing like this has happened yet as far as I can tell, but I'm not far into the histories yet."

Tanwen frowned. "Arwyne, in the fifteen years you've been the liaison, have you ever needed to crack open the histories? We do have scribes who could do the legwork."

"I know, but I don't know what to tell them to look for, or if there is anything to this. It seems odd that it's come to my attention at the same time as these mage attacks, and I don't know if I'm reading too much into it."

Tanwen returned the parchment to the table. "All right. You're going to do it your way no matter what I say. Let me know if there is anything else you need."

"There's nothing more that can be done now. I would be grateful if you would congratulate Quillon on his good timing. You saw him fly past the window, didn't you?"

"I did, and it couldn't have been better if I'd coached him."

"That thought crossed my mind. Go now, and get warmed up."

Tanwen grinned and let herself out. She wasn't cold from the short flight, but she wasn't about to turn down a chance for a hot soak.

***

As the door shut behind Tanwen, Arwyne reached out telepathically for her dragon, Vieux.

I hate telling that story. It's so misleading.

Vieux brushed her mind with sympathy. *It is the story that must be told. If they knew the whole story there would have been chaos generations ago.*

I know. But what happens if the Shunned decide to come back?

We have no proof that they lived.

She shifted in her chair to ease the throbbing in her back. *But if they did, wouldn't they harbor a grudge, especially against dragons? What if this necromancer is a Shunned descendant?*

If that is the case, we will tell the truth to those who need to know, but only if and when the time comes.

It's coming, if the seers are to be believed.

Trouble is coming, but it will not be our problem. You and I will be gone by then.

I hope you're right.

Stop fretting over that. You've missed something more important.

Tanwen knows it's not the whole story.

I haven't missed it, and she doesn't know it. She only thinks something isn't right with it.

Is that not the same thing?

Arwyne clenched her jaw. *Vieux, we have been partners for fifty years, and you haven't figured out the subtleties of human cognition?*

I lack experience. You are not subtle.

Arwyne scoffed. *That is true, but you didn't have to point it out. Anyway, I hope we're both wrong. If we're not, it means she is likely my successor, and I would wish better for her.*

She is the natural choice. Even Quillon suspects it is so. Do not fret. What you should do instead is ensure that whoever does succeed you learns the whole story. Whoever she is will need the knowledge, but you must safeguard it so only your successor discovers it.

I wonder, should I write it down? Only Raine knows it, besides you and I.

Vask knows it also.

Arwyne frowned. *Vask is alive? But he flew away years ago, after Lissa died.*

I would know if he had died. He has not. One never knows what might happen. Do what you think best.

Read more in
Dawn Before The Dark
By Wendy Blanton

**Available now
at Amazon, Barnes & Noble,
& other booksellers.**

Excerpt from the novel
Murder by the Acre
By Stephen B. Bagley

LATER LISA TOLD BERNARD it was no wonder that Mrs. DeMatt screamed, "You killed him!" After all, Lisa was kneeling over a dead man with blood on her hands.

Until that moment, the afternoon had gone pleasantly enough. Millie Sader, the day aide at the Ryton Memorial Library, returned from lunch on time for once so Librarian Bernard M. Worthington was ready to go when Mrs. DeMatt showed up. Lisa Trent pulled into the library parking lot a few minutes later. Mrs. DeMatt drove the couple around the small city of Ryton looking at various homes on the market.

"I think you'll find this next house to be really special," Mrs. DeMatt said, one hand on the steering wheel and the other handing him a paper that gave information about the home and showed a couple of photos.

"Look at this," Bernard said, turning to show the paper to Lisa who was in the center of the back seat of Mrs. DeMatt's car. "It's an underground house."

"Earth-sheltered," Mrs. DeMatt said. "That's the correct term. A home sheltered by the good earth who is mother to us all."

Bernard and Lisa exchanged an amused glance at the real estate agent's hyperbole.

"I know it's a bit more than you wanted to spend," Mrs. DeMatt said. "But quality is worth the extra expense, I always say."

They reached the earth-sheltered home around three. It was located at the edge of Ryton city limits on Watts Ridge Road. The closest home to it was nearly a mile away.

"It's almost like being in the country, but you still have the convenience of city water and sewer," Mrs. DeMatt said, flipping through her listing book to locate the home. "Let's see. It was built in the seventies during the energy crisis. As you might guess, it has very low heating and cooling bills. The savings are considerable."

"I like the idea of saving money," Bernard said.

"And it's so good that your home can conserve energy and help save the environment," Mrs. DeMatt said. "When I sell a home like

97

this, I feel like I'm doing my part."

"Isn't it dark inside?" Lisa asked. Built back into a small hill, the house reminded her of a hobbit hole. *Wonder if Bilbo is home,* she thought.

"Oh, no, not at all," Mrs. DeMatt said, leading them up the walk from the driveway. "It has these windows in the front. And it has skylights in each of the bedrooms and the master bathroom. I think that you'll be surprised at how airy and bright it is. It has such a spacious feeling." The real estate agent reached up and tried to unlock a small box fastened near the top of the door. "This doesn't...seem to want...to turn," she said. "Mr. Worthington, if you could?"

"Sure," Bernard said, taking the key from her and starting to fiddle with the box.

"I don't know why they fasten the lock-boxes so high," Mrs. DeMatt said. "I know I could turn it if it was lower."

"Maybe it keeps kids from messing with them," Bernard said. "Here it is." The lock box opened, and Bernard extracted a key from it. He handed it to the real estate agent.

"Thank you," she said. "Oh, the door is open." She frowned. "Someone forgot to lock it. I run into this all the time. The younger agents aren't as careful as they should be. That's one of the reasons so many people count on DeMatt Real Estate: They know they can depend on us to practice due diligence at all times."

Mrs. DeMatt opened the door and let Bernard and Lisa enter the home before her. "There are a few things left in the house that go with it," Mrs. DeMatt said. "When the current owner was transferred up north, he wasn't able to take everything. It's mostly living room furniture and a few things in the master bedroom." She led the way down the short entryway and turned to the left. "This is the living room."

"Wow," Bernard said.

Lisa echoed the sentiment. The living room was huge. It stretched half the length of the house. Tall windows let in light from the warm May sun. A couch, covered with a gray drop cloth, sat in the center of the room. Two small tables, also covered, nestled against it—rather like tiny puppies pressing against their mother, Lisa thought.

"Didn't I say it was spacious," Mrs. DeMatt said.

"It's certainly that," Lisa said, moving out into the room. "What could they possibly have had in here?"

"A grand piano would be about right," Bernard said. "Or maybe Rodin's Thinker."

With a quick glance at Bernard, Mrs. DeMatt said firmly, "I know it seems a little daunting, but a room this size is not meant to be a large space in itself. You can easily create conversation niches by careful arrangement of furniture and accessories. I can see one by the windows and then, of course, another toward the center of the room and a cozy arrangement by the fireplace."

Lisa nodded doubtfully, thinking it would take a lot of furniture and several plants—maybe even a tree or two—to make the room livable.

A shrill beeping sounded. Mrs. DeMatt fumbled in her purse, brought out a pager, and turned it off. "I need to call my office. I've been expecting a call from my daughter. Do you mind? You could look at the rest of the house. I'll just be a moment. I left my cell in my car." Not waiting for an answer, she bustled out the door.

Bernard and Lisa looked at each other.

"I think this is where we're supposed to wander around the house and fall in love with it," Bernard said.

"Let's do our part," Lisa said.

Bernard looked around the room. Two entrances led further into the house. "I'll take the right. It's the kitchen. Maybe they left food."

"Ah, my hunter-gatherer," Lisa said. Bernard smiled, sketched a mock salute, and marched out the door. Lisa watched him go, enjoying a warm feeling that she seemed to be experiencing often these days. She headed for the left opening, which turned out to be a hall that had four doors off it. She looked around, found the hall light switch and flipped it on, then started trying the doors. The first opened into a bathroom, and the second and third to empty bedrooms. The average size of all three rooms surprised Lisa; after the living room she had expected more. The bedrooms had frosted skylights that gave the rooms a brighter feel than Lisa had imagined. *Maybe that's just the way hobbits build things.*

She opened the fourth door. It belonged to the master bedroom, which was larger than the other bedrooms, not on the scale of the living room, but larger. A king-size bed divided the room in half and lay beneath a large frosted skylight. Lisa was surprised to see a red satin bedspread pulled back on the bed, revealing red satin sheets and red satin pillows. *Yuck. It looks like something from the Playboy school of decorating.* She heard the front door open.

Lisa stuck her head around the corner and yelled back up the hallway. "I'm back here, Mrs. DeMatt. Bernard's in the kitchen." She waited for a moment, but the real estate agent didn't appear. Lisa shrugged and walked back into the room.

Beyond the bed, an open door revealed the master bath. Lisa walked toward it. Something crunched under her shoe. She stepped back and looked down at the squashed body of a bee. It was still moving a little so she stepped on it again.

"I hope there aren't any of your friends around," she said. Bernard had told her once that bees wouldn't bother her if she didn't bother them, but she pointed out that would be fine if the bees weren't the ones who made the decision about what bothered them.

Looking to see if any bees were flying around the room, she headed for the bathroom again. Her foot caught on something. She stumbled, tried to direct her fall on the bed, but missed. She fell beside the bed on something lumpy and wet. She raised her head and realized that she had fallen on…a man! She gasped and scrambled back.

The man didn't move. Lisa's eyes traveled up his bare legs to the black satin boxers to the blood pooled on his bare back.

"Oh no oh no, not again," she said. "Bernard! Bernard! Come here!"

She carefully crawled over the man and gingerly reached out, intending to see if he was breathing.

"You killed him!" Mrs. DeMatt screamed from the doorway. "You killed him!"

Read more in

Murder by the Acre

By Stephen B. Bagley

**Available Now
at Amazon, Barnes & Noble,
and other retailers**

Excerpt from the novel
Nova Wave
By D.E. Chandler

Max

JUST AS I WAS TURNING WEST onto 166, I spotted six heavy helicopters off to the north. They were coming toward Sapulpa, flying low and slow. *Those are either ours and I don't know, or somebody else has some really big toys. Nobody should have really big toys right now but us.* At the same time, the first of the centaurs appeared in the field off to my right. I leaned into the turn and throttled her up. If I was quick, they'd lose me before the turn and I'd make the fence-line with time to spare. Just as I was finishing the turn, I saw smoke off to the north, just past the train tracks. It was coming from the farmhouse. I wanted to just keep going, but the thought that someone might still be in there made me turn up the gravel drive.

I still outran the centaurs easily, but without Arlan's wards to stop them, they got a little closer than I liked. One of them hurled a rock that whizzed by my head. As I got close to the house, they veered off and went back toward the highway. I guess the smoke scared them off. As I got closer, I also noticed that the fire was spreading quickly. If there was anyone in there, they were probably already dead. A movement out in the pole barn caught my eye. I looked just in time to see the door finish closing on the closed side. Somebody was in there, and if that fire got too close to that hay and those supports, they would be engulfed before they could get out.

When I got to the barn, I knew that if the people in there were armed they would probably shoot first and not bother asking questions. I also knew if it was a nova I stood a fair chance of getting eaten, being by myself. I knocked anyway, that way I'd know if there was someone normal there. No one answered. I turned the knob and called in. No one answered. I unholstered my .45 and nudged it open, making sure to push it all the way back to the wall. It stopped about three feet short and sprung back. Something was there. I stepped into the barn, but away from the door and kicked it, sending it crashing into whoever or whatever was back there.

A high, chortling wail issued from the area, and whoever was

101

there, moved out. Quick. They barreled out from behind the door and ducked in between the hay bales. All I could make out was that they were tall, and dressed in some kind of camouflaged armor. All browns and grays.

I followed as quickly as I dared and plastered my back against the wall outside the hay stall, ready to draw down on whoever had set fire to the house. I could see the form crouched in the far corner, but couldn't make out any details.

"You want to come out of there and you want to do it now."

There was a sort of buzzy whimper from the area. And whoever it was shifted and appeared to cower more. I wasn't getting anything from them in the way of anger or malice. In fact, they felt pretty scared.

"I won't hurt you if you come out now and let me see you," I said, though probably still with a little too much command in my voice. I tried shifting tactics. I laid my gun on the dining room table, just within reach if I needed it, and tried to project calm, curiosity, and helpfulness. "Look," I said, "No gun. Come on out, let's have a look at you. Are you hurt?"

I edged a little closer to the table then, as first one long appendage and then another stood up from the cowering form. Then there was a head. Attached to it were the two appendages. They were ears. Two long—er, well, tall ears standing straight up off of a slightly humanish face. It was a furry face—mostly. There were what looked like chitinous plates coming from around the back of the head and under the ears, but also up over the top of the head, between the ears. Then there were the great big camel brown eyes and the busy, snuffling nose.

Enchanted, I urged it to come out further. The critter stood slowly, still very cautious, and when it reached full height those ears came very close to the eight-foot ceiling. Before me stood a six-foot-plus jackrabbit-grasshopper nova clutching what looked like a kid's baseball hat.

I cursed under my breath and said, "Hey. You got a name there, fella?"

The creature stared at me, those eyes unfathomable, though his fear did seem to be subsiding a little. It seemed to be contemplating whether I was going to be okay after all. I'd just given up on any kind of answer, when it spoke and nearly had me on the floor.

"Fixx."

"Is that your house, Fixx? I managed after a moment.

"Fixx," he said matter of factly.

"You just got the one word, huh?"

"Fixx," again, with all the inflection he could muster with just the one word, to indicate his disappointment. I did very much get the feeling he was a male. A male what, though? That chitinous armor extended down in segments to allow movement, but it formed a collar and breastplate, and then hung down his back in great long wing covers. His front legs (arms?) were furry, and appeared to possess the usual number of phalanges and an opposable thumb of sorts. The hindquarters were more insect than mammal, plated and jointed very much like the grasshopper he resembled. At the very back of the assemblage was a short, twitchy furry tail. Longer than a cotton tail, and slightly prehensile, if my eyes weren't fooling me.

"Did you see what happened over there?"

"Fixx."

"You want to come with me and help out?"

"Fixx!"

Those big ears twitched forward and the only thing coming from him now was joy. I turned and went back out to the yard and Fixx followed me out. Once he got out of the pole barn, he stretched to his full height. The dude was at least eight feet tall, without the ears. I wondered how he was going to fit on the bike. I got on and realized that even if he fit, there wouldn't be any room for me.

"I'll go slow," I said, "So you can keep up."

He made a chittering sound and watched as I eased out of the parking lot. I was watching him and going slow, but I was nearly to The Office's gravel drive before he made a move. When he did, it was sudden. I watched in my rearview as those back legs cranked tight and then let loose, flinging all eight feet of rabbit-bug through the air like a crossbow bolt. I almost lost sight of him completely he moved so fast.

He had not only hopped, but had opened a set of luminous, iridescent wings from under his wing covers. He hovered a moment and then set down just outside of Arlan's wards. I motioned for him to follow, and he reluctantly stepped forward. He seemed to shudder as he stepped through, but suffered no ill effects that I could see. I nodded to the tree-girl as we went up the hill. He followed me up to the barn, and the short, hoodie-wearing valets I called jawas were all eyes as he sniffed around the base of the barn that covered the entrance to the building. I just stood and watched him sniff around. *What am I gonna do with you?*

The centaurs wouldn't cross Arlan's charms, but Fixx had crossed them, if cautiously. Wards, Arlan had called them, but they reminded me of Mama Vierna's barrier charms. The jawas eventually walked my bike to the back where the construction crew was just finishing the parking garage in the side of the hill summit. When they were done, we'd be able to drive in, get out, and the vehicle would be driven through into a camouflaged entrance in the top of the hill. From where I stood in the barn, the cars would simply seem to drive out and vanish.

I opened the little door that had once led to the tack room, and felt the faint electric crackle of the next barrier give way, revealing the deceptively simple-looking wooden trap door. It took several minutes for Fixx to decide to follow me in. I hefted the trap door open and started my descent of the thirteen flights of stairs to the bottom. I was halfway down before I heard Fixx start his descent. Best to let him come in his own time and in his own way.

Upon reaching the first floor of The Office of Human Protection, I pushed through the stainless-steel blast door into the beige hallway. Well, most of it was beige. Several large braziers had been set along the walls to light them, and they did produce rather large spots of soot above them. Hopefully, we'd have our solar panels installed soon, and the braziers would be retired. They stank to high heaven, but they did give the place a cool dungeon-y feel. Arlan greeted me as I pushed open the double doors at the end of the hallway into the commons.

"Maxwell! How is it out there? Did you find me any flippers?"

"Not this time," I said, glancing at his now-worn flip-flops, and offering the elder dude a grin, "I'll see what they've got left at the Glenpool Great-Mart when Daniel and I make our next run this afternoon. Hey, I did catch sight of a group of heavy choppers though. Any idea what that's about?"

"No," he said, his tone ominous, "but Toni might." Then he went to exit the commons, and stopped, eyes wide. I had to suppress a grin, knowing what he must have thought seeing Fixx. I could feel the impact of the surprise as it took him, followed by unmistakable awe.

He was still staring when I went back out to collect Fixx and guide him into the commons.

"She's in town and so is Dr. Pape. Going to try and recruit Ellen."

"Ah, good." He still stared at Fixx.

"She's just a kid. And she's been injured. She doesn't need to be going out and facing these things." That seemed to snap him out of it.

"Perhaps, my boy, she's stronger than you think. I really do feel very strongly about her importance. Of course, she will have the ultimate say in her future."

"I hope so," I said, pulling one of the folding chairs out from the first row of tables in the mess area. "I kind of think she's important too, but you know, it's like everything I touch turns to shit."

"You shouldn't keep those kinds of feelings." He sat down directly across from me. "You know that they get stuck in there and cause you problems. How are you doing with controlling the empathy?" Fixx didn't sit, but hunkered down a bit at the end of the table. He was still looking around, twitching that nose and those whiskers, taking it all in.

"It's a little better," I said, "but it feels like the more I try to control it the more it grows. And sometimes it seems like I'm still projecting without noticing it. Thank the gods there's a proximity factor. Otherwise—"

"You just keep working with it. We're going to be relying heavily on what you and Daniel can do in days to come. Any word on the arrival of your Mama Vierna?"

"She's due in on the Carolina caravan next week. It's stressing me out, but I'm sure she can hold her own. Hell, she was practicing voodoo since before I was born."

"Wonderful. I look forward to meeting her. It'll be nice to meet another practitioner with experience." He inhaled deeply. The smell of sweet potatoes and some sort of roast fowl seemed to soothe him, and his face relaxed into a smile of contentment. He patted his round belly through the material of his Hawaiian shirt. He looked to be completely in his element.

"Well, that must be lunch," I said, and I headed for the line that was forming. Arlan was only a step behind me. His excitement registered on my "empathic palette" and I did what I could to shift the energetic barrier to block the emotions of all of the people in the line and the servers. It left my three o'clock less protected, but there was only one person that way. I hadn't paid any attention to who it was.

His guilt and sorrow hit me so hard I grabbed the tray rail along the hot bar. My knees buckled, and Arlan grabbed my elbow. I tried shifting my energy barrier back to intercept it, but all I could do was hold on and sob. Arlan's alarm caused a commotion at the mess line, and whoever it was in the shadows of my three-o'clock grew self-conscious and left.

As the emotion faded from my palette, I was able to straighten up and move down the line. Still, there were great big tears on my face, and a remnant sob or two before I could speak. It was embarrassing. It made me angry. I went through the line as quickly as possible, allowing the servers to pile whatever they wanted to on my tray, then collected it and went straight back out the double doors into the empty hallway.

Read more in

Nova Wave

By D. E. Chandler

**Available now
at Amazon, Barnes & Noble,
& other booksellers.**

ABOUT THE AUTHORS

Kathy Akins began writing as a teenager, but serious pursuit of the craft started when she retired from a 30-year career with the United States Postal Service. She has won several awards with her poetry, articles, and short fiction. Her short stories, memoirs, poetry, and devotionals were published in *Blackbirds Third Flight*, *Prosateurs: Tales & Truth*, and *Yule Tidings*. A love for history, family, and animals touches her everyday life and inspires her story ideas and characters. She lives in Oklahoma and shares her home with miniature longhair dachshunds. She is a member of Prosateurs, Society of Children's Book Writers and Illustrators, and American Christian Fiction Writers. Visit her website at *kathyakins.blogspot.com*.

Debbie Anderson wrote the suspense novel *Friend or Foe*, and recently published *Lizzie*, a story for pre-teens and young adults. A long-time storyteller, she has written and shared stories since she was a child. The oldest of eight children she used these stories to entertain her siblings as well for her own enjoyment. She learned the love of travel going on family vacations and spent eighteen years in the travel industry. As a result, she has been to nearly every state and six countries. She left the travel business after 9/11. Since then she has written business documents such as manuals and procedures for the electronic and oil industries. In addition to writing, she enjoys sewing, quilting, crafts, painting, and spending time with her family, especially her grandchildren. She finds humor in everyday people and events and incorporates them into her writing. She writes short stories, memoirs, novels, children's stories, and how-to books. She is a member of Prosateurs, Oklahoma Writers Federation Inc., Ada Writers, and Writing for Fun. She has been published in the Creations anthologies, *Yule Tidings*, *Prosateurs: Tales & Truth*, and other publications.

Stephen B. Bagley's latest book is *Floozy Comes Back*, a collection of humorous essays. He co-wrote *Undying*, a collection of poetry. He wrote the cozy mysteries *Murder by Dewey Decimal* and *Murder by the Acre*. His other books include *Tales from Bethlehem, Floozy and Other Stories*, and *EndlesS*. He wrote the full-length plays *Murder at the Witch's Cottage* and *Two Writers in the Hands of an Angry God* and co-wrote *Turnabout*. His poetry, articles, short stories, and essays have appeared in *Yule Tidings, Writer's Digest, Blackbirds First Flight, Blackbirds Second Flight, Blackbirds Third Flight, ByLine Magazine, Nautilus Magazine, Prosateurs: Tales & Truth, Pontotoc County Chronicles, Tulsa World OKMagazine, Free Star*, the Creations anthologies 2012-2015, and other print and online publications. He graduated from Oklahoma State University, Stillwater, Oklahoma, with a Bachelor of Science in Journalism. He is a member of Oklahoma Writers Federation, Inc., Christian Indie Writers, 10 Minute Novelists, Real Authors, and the founding president of Prosateurs. Visit his website at *stephenbbagley.blogspot.com*.

Wendy Blanton started writing when she learned to string words into sentences. She is the author of The Balphrahn trilogy. The first book, *Dawn Before The Dark*, is available now. Her short stories and articles have been published in *Yule Tidings, Prosateurs: Tales & Truth, Blackbirds First Flight, Blackbirds Second Flight*, and *Blackbirds Third Flight*. Currently, she writes epic fantasy novels and short stories. She has a Bachelor of Applied Science in Business Management from the University of Mount Olive, Mount Olive, North Carolina, and served on active duty for the United States Air Force for eight years. When she isn't writing, she can usually be found in her garden or puttering in the kitchen. She lives in Missouri with her husband and cats. She is a member of Realm Makers Consortium and Oklahoma Writers Federation, Inc. and a founding member of Prosateurs. Visit her website at *wendyblanton.com*.

D.E. Chandler wrote the Nova Wave series, which includes *Nova Wave* and *Bone Silver*. Her book *Weathered* gathers her short stories and poetry in her first collection. Her poem, "Oppenheimer" and short story "One Way Window" won honorable mention and publication in *Outside the Lines*. Her poem "Carroll After Dark" won first place and publication in a *Tulsa Review*'s Spring contest issue. Her short story "LiveLash Challenge" was published in Ghostlight Magazine. Her other short stories, poems, photographs, essays, and articles have been published in *Yule Tidings, Prosateurs: Tales & Truth, Blackbirds Third Flight, The Green Country Guardian, Sapulpa Herald*, and *Sapulpa News and Views*. She received her Master of Fine Arts from Oklahoma City University, Oklahoma. She lives with her husband Tom in Oklahoma. She is a member of Horror Writers Association, Oklahoma Writers Federation, Inc., and a founding member of Prosateurs. Visit her website at *dechandlerwrites.com*.

Heath Stallcup was born in Salinas, California, and relocated to Oklahoma in his teen years. He joined the US Navy and was stationed in Charleston, South Carolina, and Bangor, Washington, shortly after junior college. After his second tour, he attended East Central University, Ada, Oklahoma, where he obtained Bachelor of Science degrees in Biology and Chemistry. He then served ten years with the State of Oklahoma as a Compliance and Enforcement Officer while moonlighting nights and weekends with the local sheriff's office. He and his wife live in rural Oklahoma. His books include: *Whispers of the Past, Forneus Corson, Flags of the Forgotten, Burning Bridges*, the *Monster Squad* series, the *Caldera* series, the *Nocturna* series, and the *Hunter* series. His short stories have been published in several print and online anthologies. Visit his website at *heathstallcup.com*.

Joanne Verbridge was born in Oakland, California, spending her early life experiences in Northern California. Family brought her to Oklahoma where she enjoys writing memoirs and crafting. She works to inspire her young nieces and other youth people to take an interest in storytelling and writing. She is a member of Oklahoma Writers Federation, Inc., and a founding member of Prosateurs. Her memoirs, short stories, and articles have been published in newspapers, *Yule Tidings, Prosateurs: Tales & Truth,* and the Creations anthologies.

Dawn Before The Dark
By Wendy Blanton

An ancient curse keeps men in fear of dragons, so only women can ride them in Slan—while only men can perform magic. As a necromancer from beyond the edge of the known world threatens invasion, Briant appears—a young man who loves dragons.

Wybren Tanwen must decide: Is Briant the one who is the dragon-born, the fulfillment of prophecy?

Will he save Slan? Or destroy it?

First book in The Balphrahn series.

On Sale Now!

Friend or Foe
By Debbie Anderson

Janie is your average college-aged girl with her future ahead of her. Her quirky personality includes her love of old music and movies, she talks to herself, and she often finds herself in unusual situations. She loves her job and has lots of good friends. Life is great! Then she accidentally hits a policeman with a bagel!

Romance blossoms. A black truck with tinted windows is following her. She doesn't know who it is, but it continues to stalk her. How can she get her life back? Who is in the truck? Is it *Friend or Foe*?

ON SALE NOW!

Murder by the Acre
By Stephen B. Bagley

The intrepid librarian and roving reporter return! This time Bernard M. Worthington and Lisa Trent stumble upon the body of a local jeweler and ladies man in an underground house. As the couple and Police Chief Chuck Donaldson investigate, they soon find themselves entangled in a confusing mystery of lies and alibis that involves the upper crust of Ryton, Oklahoma.

Who murdered him, and how and why was he killed? Why doesn't the widow care that her husband is dead? Why doesn't his mistress? What does the mysterious Aventura Corporation have to do with the murder? Soon events spiral out of control as the killer strikes again and again. As the three dig for the truth, they upset powerful, vengeful people. The chief might lose his job, but Bernard and Lisa could lose their lives in this suspenseful sequel to *Murder by Dewey Decimal*.

On Sale Now!

NOCTURNA
By Heath Stallcup

The 21st century brought more plagues to mankind than any other time in history. Some were created by man; others were acts of God. Even Mother Nature herself turned against the infestation known as man.

Nearly thirty percent of the population was killed by new virus strains. Racial tensions flared and evolved into two civil wars. Nations fragmented into numerous 'no-go' combat zones controlled by local warlords, most still active to this day.

At a time when mankind should have been reaching for the future, it devolved into a nearly apocalyptic present, pitting neighbor against neighbor and nation against nation until another twenty percent of the world's population had been extinguished.

Then came the asteroid Wormwood. And everything changed...for the worse.

ON SALE NOW!

Nova Wave
By D.E. Chandler

The Office of Human Protection has come to small-town Oklahoma, but the situation is anything but stable. When agents go missing, Maxwell Edison must investigate.

When Max goes missing and a coup is staged from within, everything depends on a woman waking up in a changed world.

A woman who has suffered a grievous injury.

A woman with no training...

Can she possibly save him?

ON SALE NOW!

Prosateurs: Tales & Truth

Enjoy articles, devotionals, essays, memoirs, recipes, short stories, and more from these authors:

Kathy Akins
Debbie Anderson
Stephen B. Bagley
Kelley Benson
Nita Beshear
Wendy Blanton
D.E. Chandler
Barbara Shepherd
Joanne Verbridge

ON SALE NOW!

Yule Tidings

Celebrate Thanksgiving, Christmas & New Year's with these articles, devotionals, essays, memoirs, recipes and short stories from these authors:

Kathy Akins
Debbie Anderson
Stephen B. Bagley
Wendy Blanton
D.E. Chandler
Barbara Shepherd
Joanne Verbridge

ON SALE NOW!